"My daughter is none of your business!" Joe informed Savanna.

"It's pretty obvious she isn't yours, either," Savanna answered back.

"Just what are you implying, Ms. Starr?"

"I'm implying that when daddy lessons were given, you must have been absent for the whole course!"

"And just what makes you an authority on fathering?"

"I was a teenage girl once, just like Megan. And I know what it feels like to be in a strange city without friends or anyone to talk to."

"And just what am I?" he shot back.

Savanna's lips twisted mockingly. "You don't really want me to answer that, Mr. McCann."

He didn't know what it was about her that got to him. Even when she was angry and impertinent and saying things to him that no other woman had ever dared say, he wanted to kiss her. She was like a beautiful little wildcat that he desperately wanted to tame....

Dear Reader,

This month, Silhouette Romance has an exciting lineup for you—perfect reading for these warm, romantic summer nights—starting with a new BUNDLES OF JOY title from Kristin Morgan. In *Make Room for Baby,* a new arrival brings Camille Boudreaux and Bram Delcambre together as a family—and gives their lost love a second chance.

Stella Bagwell brings her heartwarming style to the FABULOUS FATHERS series with *Daddy Lessons.* Joe McCann was about to fire Savanna Starr until he saw her skill at child rearing. But would helping this single dad raise his teenage daughter lead to a new job—as his wife?

Another irresistible cowboy meets his match in the latest WRANGLERS & LACE title, *Wildcat Wedding.* Look for this tale of Western loving by Patricia Thayer.

As for the rest of the month, you'll be SPELLBOUND by Sandra Paul's humorous tale of a very determined angel and the very stubborn bachelor she tries to reform in *His Accidental Angel.* Charlotte Moore brings a *Belated Bride* back to her hometown to face the man who left her at the altar. And Judith Janeway makes her debut this month with a charming and humorous love story, *A Convenient Arrangement.*

Happy Reading!

Anne Canadeo
Senior Editor

Please address questions and book requests to:
Silhouette Reader Service
U.S.: 3010 Walden Ave., P.O. Box 1325, Buffalo, NY 14269
Canadian: P.O. Box 609, Fort Erie, Ont. L2A 5X3

DADDY LESSONS

Stella Bagwell

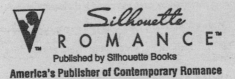

Silhouette
R O M A N C E™
Published by Silhouette Books
America's Publisher of Contemporary Romance

To Carmen and Jason,
may your life together always
be filled with love and laughter.

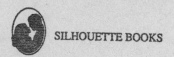

SILHOUETTE BOOKS

ISBN 0-373-19085-9

DADDY LESSONS

Copyright © 1995 by Stella Bagwell

All rights reserved. Except for use in any review, the reproduction
or utilization of this work in whole or in part in any form by any
electronic, mechanical or other means, now known or hereafter
invented, including xerography, photocopying and recording, or in
any information storage or retrieval system, is forbidden without
the written permission of the editorial office, Silhouette Books,
300 East 42nd Street, New York, NY 10017 U.S.A.

All characters in this book have no existence outside the imagination of
the author and have no relation whatsoever to anyone bearing the same
name or names. They are not even distantly inspired by any individual
known or unknown to the author, and all incidents are pure invention.

This edition published by arrangement with Harlequin Enterprises B.V.

® and TM are trademarks of Harlequin Enterprises B.V., used under
license. Trademarks indicated with ® are registered in the United States
Patent and Trademark Office, the Canadian Trade Marks Office and in
other countries.

Printed in U.S.A.

Books by Stella Bagwell

Silhouette Romance

Golden Glory #469
Moonlight Bandit #485
A Mist on the Mountain #510
Madeleine's Song #543
The Outsider #560
The New Kid in Town #587
Cactus Rose #621
Hillbilly Heart #634
Teach Me #657
The White Night #674
No Horsing Around #699
That Southern Touch #723
Gentle as a Lamb #748
A Practical Man #789
Precious Pretender #812
Done to Perfection #836
Rodeo Rider #878
*Their First Thanksgiving #903
*The Best Christmas Ever #909
*New Year's Baby #915
Hero in Disguise #954
Corporate Cowgirl #991
Daniel's Daddy #1020
A Cowboy for Christmas #1052
Daddy Lessons #1085

* Heartland Holidays Trilogy

STELLA BAGWELL

lives in the rural mountains of southeastern Oklahoma where she enjoys the wildlife and hikes in the woods with her husband. She has a son, a wonderful daughter-in-law and a great passion for writing romances—a job she hopes to keep for a long time to come. Many of Stella's books have been transcribed to audiotapes for the Oklahoma Library for the Blind. She hopes her blind audience, and all her readers, will continue to enjoy her stories.

Joe McCann on Fatherhood...

Dear Megan,

For ten years I had to watch you grow through only snapshots and weekend visits. Then the unexpected chance came for me to be your full-time father, and I was thrilled at the prospect of having my daughter back in my life again.

When you moved into the house with your loud rock music, messy room and headstrong attitude, I was lost. I realized I didn't know how to be a father. Much less a father to a precocious teenage daughter. All I knew was that I loved you and wanted you to be happy.

Then Savanna stepped in and taught me that being a father didn't necessarily mean seeing that you went to private school or trying to give you the very best of everything. It simply meant loving you. And I do, my little darling. I do.

Daddy

Chapter One

Savanna Starr furiously pumped the handle of the hydraulic jack and tried to ignore the honks of the traffic whizzing by her. She was fully aware that she and her Volkswagen Beetle were creating a road hazard. But, darn it, I-40 in downtown Oklahoma City wasn't blessed with a lot of shoulder to safely park on, and she could hardly keep driving with a tire that resembled a black pancake!

Even though it wasn't yet eight in the morning, the June sun was unbelievably hot. As she worked to jack the little car off its back left wheel, Savanna could feel perspiration popping out beneath her linen shift, on her brow and upper lip.

Great, just great, she muttered to herself. By the time she got to her new job she was going to be covered with sweat and grease. What was her boss going to think?

Never mind that, she told herself as she hurriedly grabbed the spare tire from the trunk and heaved it to the ground. What was he going to say if, God forbid, she was late?

* * *

Joe McCann poured himself a cup of coffee from the pot he'd brewed forty minutes ago, then peeped through the slatted blinds on the window.

Where was she? It was fifteen minutes past eight. Joe knew his full-time secretary, Edie, had clearly informed the temporary service that he expected the new girl to be here in the office at eight. That didn't mean fifteen after!

Hell, he snorted to himself as he sank back into a leather desk chair. He should have interviewed the woman himself. Now, while Edie was away on maternity leave, he was going to have to put up with some irresponsible nitwit in the office for six long weeks. With a pile of worries already on his mind, he didn't know how he could deal with that, too.

McCann Drilling, the company his late father had built from the ground up, was crying for business. And then there was Megan, his thirteen-year-old daughter. She'd only been back in his life for less than a week now and he was learning what it was like to be a full-time parent all over again.

Damn it all, he silently cursed, a lax secretary was the last thing he needed!

Three miles away, Savanna tossed the lug wrench in with the dilapidated tire and hydraulic jack, slammed the trunk, then jumped back into the driver's seat. She couldn't believe her luck. A flat tire and not one person had stopped to offer her a helping hand. She'd strained and tugged at least ten minutes just to loosen the lug nuts. So much for chivalry these days!

After a quick glance over her shoulder, Savanna merged the little orange car back into the heavy stream of traffic, then jammed the accelerator all the way to the floor. She wasn't worried about getting a speeding ticket. Right now she was more concerned about Joe McCann. According to his secretary, he was a stickler for punctuality.

The thought dared Savanna to glance at her wristwatch. What she saw made her wail loud enough to drown out the rock music playing on the radio. "I'm twenty minutes late! I'm going to be fired before I ever go to work!"

Back at the McCann Drilling office, Joe got up from his desk, tossed the remainder of his coffee into the trash, then began to pace around the sparsely furnished room. He didn't like waiting for anyone or anything. It was a waste of time.

His mother had often told him that he needed to be more patient with people. And Joe figured that was probably true now that he was trying to deal with his daughter. But he'd always lived his life by hard discipline. He didn't know how to be patient with his employees or his daughter.

The thought of Megan had him pausing by the corner of his desk where her photo sat smiling up at him. He hated to admit it, but he didn't know her. At least, not in the ways that really counted. But since his divorce ten years ago he'd been forced to watch her grow up through snapshots and brief weekends spent together in the summer months.

Then a month ago he'd been surprised by a call from his ex-wife, Deirdre. Her husband's job was taking them to Africa and she believed it would be best for Megan to remain in the States and live with her father.

Joe had been quick to agree. He hadn't wanted his daughter in a country where civil unrest was rampant and living conditions less than ideal, to say the least. Moreover, for years he'd wanted full custody of his daughter and he wasn't about to pass up the chance.

But so far, having Megan living under the same roof with him was nothing like he'd expected it to be. Fathering a teenage girl around the clock was like handling a stick of dynamite. One wrong word brought on an explosion. And most of the time he was the one doing the exploding!

The squeal of brakes and the slam of a car door brought Joe out of his thoughts. Quickly he walked over to the window and glanced out the blinds.

An orange Volkswagen Beetle was parked next to his pickup truck. No one was in the ancient little car, and he could only guess that the blond woman streaking up the sidewalk to the front entrance of the building had been the driver.

Could that have been his new secretary? Surely not! She'd looked like a teenager!

Joe sat at his desk, but before he had time to consider that horrible idea the tapping of high heels sounded outside in the corridor, then a softer knock came at the door.

Leaning up in his seat, Joe sucked in a bracing breath, then folded his hands atop the walnut desk.

"Come in," he called.

Dear Lord, was that her boss's voice? Savanna swallowed nervously, then forced herself to reach for the doorknob. Even if the man sounded like a grizzly bear, she couldn't stay out here in the corridor, she scolded herself.

After wiping her sweaty palms down her hips, Savanna slowly turned the knob and pushed open the door. Yet before she could step inside, a male voice barked loudly.

"I said come in!"

The unexpected summons caused Savanna to practically jump over the threshold and into the office.

"Good morning," she said in a breathless rush to the man staring at her from behind a wide desk. "I'm Savanna Starr. The temporary help. Are you Mr. Joe McCann?"

He nodded, then stood. Savanna's eyes followed his movements and she was instantly struck by his tall, muscular body, thick, tawny blond hair and piercing blue eyes.

"I am," he said brusquely. "And you're late. Did you know you were supposed to be here at eight o'clock?"

Color flooded Savanna's cheeks, but she bravely held his gaze. Dear Lord, she thought with surprise, Joe McCann was a young man! She hadn't expected that. How many men in their mid-thirties were capable of drilling for gas or oil, much less owning their own drilling company? She'd been expecting an old man with gray hair and a pot belly. Joe McCann wasn't anything like that. He was—all man!

Finally managing to unglue her tongue from the roof of her mouth, she said, "Yes, sir, I did. But—"

"I don't like tardiness, Ms. Starr."

Carefully, she placed her purse and lunch sack on the floor beside her feet, then straightened before she spoke. "Neither do I, Mr. McCann," she said in her most crisp, businesslike voice. "But unfortunately it couldn't be helped. You see, I—"

"Save the explanations," he interrupted. "You should have started earlier."

Before Savanna could stop it, a gasp of disbelief rushed past her lips. She needed this job. But did she really want to work for a man who was looking at her as if he'd never seen a woman before? Much less a woman who had happened to commit the evil sin of being late? What sort of man was he, anyway?

Feeling an unusual spurt of temper, Savanna decided to damn the consequences and speak her mind. "For your information, Mr. McCann, I did start early. But I had a flat tire on I-40. Do you know how many big, strong, macho men like you stopped to help me?"

Joe's eyebrows shot up as Savanna Starr impatiently tapped the toe of her beige high heel. Obviously she was waiting for his answer, but he could only stare at her. He'd never seen anything like this woman.

When he didn't immediately respond, Savanna felt inclined to go on before she lost her nerve. "I'll tell you, Mr. McCann. Not one stopped to give me a hand. I guess they all had bosses like you and were afraid of being late themselves."

Joe's lips parted, but still he didn't say anything. He was too busy trying to figure out what a woman like her was doing in his office. She didn't look anything like a secretary. And as far as he was concerned, she wasn't behaving like one, either. What had he done to deserve this? he wondered as frustration poured through him. First Megan and now Savanna Starr. A man couldn't be expected to deal with two unpredictable females in his life at the same time. It would be impossible. Pure hell, in fact.

From the grim expression on Joe McCann's face, Savanna knew it was too late to worry about making a first impression on him. She'd opened her big fat mouth before she could stop herself and now he couldn't get rid of her fast enough.

Well, that was the story of her life, Savanna thought miserably. Until a few months ago she'd hopped from one town and one state to the next. Her jobs had been mixed, some of them several weeks here, or a few short days there. Here today and gone tomorrow. That was the way things went for Savanna Starr. But this time it looked as if she'd be moving on even faster than usual. Like in a matter of minutes!

"Oh, brother," she groaned aloud as she glanced down at the dress she was wearing. The plain linen sheath was the color of a spring daffodil and had been one of her very favorites. Now grease marks striped her hips where she'd inadvertently wiped her dirty hands. "Looks like I've ruined my dress along with my chance for this job. I guess today just wasn't my day."

Picking up her purse and lunch sack, she turned toward the door. "I'll tell the service to send you someone else. I'm sure they can have a secretary here for you within the hour. Goodbye, Mr. McCann."

She was about to step into the hallway when the telephone began to ring. Joe's eyes jerked over to the jangling instrument. God help him, it was probably Megan already. He couldn't deal with another twenty or so calls from her again today. Before he could consider his actions, he reached out and grabbed Savanna's arm.

"Where do you think you're going?" he asked her.

What did he care? she wondered. He obviously didn't want her services. And even though she'd been excited about taking this job, she wasn't completely sure she wanted to work for Joe McCann. He not only angered her, he disturbed her in a primal sort of way. She wanted to lash out at him. Not as an offended employee. But as a woman. Which didn't make sense. She didn't know this man. So why was he getting under her skin?

"I think I'm going down to Lilly's," she finally answered.

Joe looked as blank as if Savanna had said she was headed to the moon. Behind them the telephone continued to ring.

"Pardon me, did you say Lilly's?"

Even though Savanna was annoyed with him, she decided to explain anyway. "You know where Lilly's is, don't you? That little bakery down on the corner. She has great apple fritters and since I had to miss breakfast this morning, I think I'll indulge myself. Who gives a damn about sugar and fat? I won't get to wear this dress again anyway."

"Ms. Starr!" he practically shouted. "Did I dismiss you?"

Savanna's chin tilted a fraction higher. She'd never been fired from a job in her life. But if this man was going to make a big issue of terminating her chance to work here, she wished he'd get it over with and let her be on her way. "Not verbally. But—"

His face darkened with color. "Oh, I see," he drawled mockingly. "Along with your secretarial skills you also read minds. I guess the temporary service forgot to tell me that."

Savanna couldn't ever remember meeting any man as obnoxious as Joe McCann. Which was really too bad, she thought. He had the rough sort of looks that turned women's heads. And she'd be lying if she didn't admit to herself that just for a second, when she'd walked through the door, he'd turned hers. His tall, well-muscled body was without an ounce of fat. His face was lean, too, with strong, bony features and eyes as blue as a western sky.

But Savanna wasn't in the market for a man. Especially a man like this one, who looked as though he rarely smiled, if ever. No, she'd tried romance before and her young heart had wound up shattered. She wasn't ready, or brave enough, to set herself up for that kind of pain again.

"I'm sorry to disappoint you, but I don't read minds, Mr. McCann. However, I can read faces. And at the moment I'd say yours looks about as happy as a hound with a flea on its back."

Joe rubbed his fingers against his throbbing temples. The woman might be an irresponsible oddball, but she'd certainly gotten that much right. "What did you come here for in the first place?"

His voice had suddenly gone weary and dull. As Savanna watched him scrub his face with both hands, she wondered if he was physically ill. Could that account for his waspish attitude?

"I came here to work. But I thought—"

"I believe it would be safer for both of us if you didn't think, Ms. Starr!"

Savanna's teeth ground together. She'd be crazy to be concerned about the man. He wasn't ill. He was an ass! Still, she couldn't entirely ignore the desperation in his eyes or the fatigue on his face. It was plain to her the man needed help—he just didn't quite know it yet.

Thankfully, the telephone finally quieted. Joe dropped his hold on her arm and took a step back. He didn't know why he'd grabbed hold of her in the first place. Normally he wouldn't lay a hand on any employee. Particularly a woman. But something about Savanna Starr was making him act totally out of character.

Tingling from his touch, Savanna stared at him, her mind spinning as she watched him rake a hand through his wavy blond hair.

"Are you suggesting you still want me?" she asked incredulously.

Joe's blue gaze swept over her petite but very shapely form. Savanna Starr. What kind of name was that? he wondered. It sounded like something a damn Hollywood producer would make up.

Walking over to his desk, he glanced back at her to see she was still standing in the middle of the room, staring at him with eyes the color of a fawn's coat in summer. He'd never seen such rich brown eyes on a blonde before, but then Joe rarely looked at women that closely. Since he and Deirdre had divorced, he hadn't had the time or the urge to involve himself with a woman. McCann Drilling took all his attention, and he figured that was the way it always would be. "If you think—"

Before he could go on, the telephone began to ring again. Grimacing, he motioned with his hand for Savanna to answer it. "Get that. And if it's my daughter, Megan, tell her I'm out in the work yard and that I can't talk to her now!"

Savanna quickly walked over to the desk and picked up the telephone.

"McCann Drilling," she said cheerfully. "May I help you?"

"Who are you?" A young female voice blurted the question.

Savanna glanced uncertainly at Joe McCann. Right now she didn't know if she was a secretary or an unemployed mediator.

"I'm Savanna."

"Oh, you're the one who's taking Edie's place?"

"That's right. And who are you?"

"I'm Megan. Joe is my daddy. I need to talk to him."

Obviously the girl had been forewarned there would be a change in secretaries at her father's office, Savanna concluded. "Well, Megan, right now your father is unable to come to the telephone. Perhaps I can help?"

The young girl let out a huge sigh of frustration. "I doubt it. But I guess I could tell you, anyway. I want to go to the library, but Ophelia, the housekeeper, isn't here this morning. She won't be here until two this afternoon! And I'm only thirteen. I'm not old enough to drive."

"Oh, I see. Well, you are in a fix, aren't you? I don't suppose you'd settle for watching some videos until the housekeeper is there to take you?"

Megan groaned loudly. "What videos? Joe—I mean, Daddy doesn't even have a VCR. He's old-fashioned and says time spent in front of the TV isn't productive."

Savanna couldn't help but smile at the girl's imitation of her father's voice. "Perhaps you could walk, Megan. Is it very far from your house?"

"Eight blocks," she said glumly. "But Daddy would never let me walk. He says it's too dangerous for kids to walk on the streets nowadays. Especially for a girl."

Savanna dared another glance at Joe McCann and was surprised to see he'd skirted around the desk to stand beside her. At the moment he was shaking his head and mouthing the word *no*. Savanna couldn't believe he was being so overprotective. It wasn't as if the girl was a kindergartner!

"That's true in many cases," Savanna said, careful not to go against anything her father might have already instructed her. "But if you had a friend to walk with you, then he might consider it."

She looked up to see Joe still shaking his head. A burst of anger suddenly spurted through Savanna. Didn't the man remember what it was like to be thirteen years old, out of school on summer vacation and stuck in the house alone with nothing to do?

"Well, I just came here to live with Daddy last week. So I don't really know many people," she said, then suddenly her small, dispirited voice brightened. "But there is someone I've made friends with. Cindy. She's my age and lives across the street. She'd want to go with me!"

If Megan had just now come to live with her father, Savanna mused, that could only mean Joe McCann was widowed or divorced. She didn't know why that bit of news should strike a nerve in her, but it did. So did the lost, lonely sound in Megan's voice. Savanna knew what it was like to be in a strange place surrounded by unfamiliar things and people she didn't know. Joe McCann probably didn't understand that. But Savanna did. She'd spent her whole life living in places where she felt as if she didn't belong and that no one cared whether she was around or not. In fact, she was still searching for that place she could call her real home.

"Tell you what, Megan. As soon as your father comes back in the office, I'll talk to him about it. In the meantime, why don't you call Cindy and see if she can go."

"Gee, thanks, Savanna. And please beg him if you have to. I can't stay in this dreary old house all day!"

Begging Joe McCann was the last thing Savanna intended to do. Aloud, she told Megan, "I'll do my best. 'Bye, now."

"So where is Megan wanting to trot off to now?" Joe demanded the moment Savanna hung up the phone. "You should have told her an emphatic no."

Then why didn't you answer the phone and give her a no yourself? Savanna wanted to ask him. Instead, she bit her tongue and tried to be pleasant. "Do you want her to keep calling back and asking?"

Joe rubbed a weary hand across the back of his neck. He had to admit the woman had a point. "From the time Megan moved in with me last week, she's called me constantly here at work. I can't get anything done and when I point this out to her, she bursts into tears and accuses me of not loving her."

Poor little girl, Savanna thought sadly. She must be miserable. "Do you love her?" Savanna couldn't help asking.

Joe stared at her as if she belonged in a mental institution instead of his office. "What the hell kind of question is that? Of course I love her. She's my daughter!"

Her question had offended him, but it was obvious to Savanna that this man needed some daddy lessons in the worst kind of way. "And just because she's your daughter, she's supposed to know that?"

He shot her a look that said she was inching onto dangerous ground. Savanna decided she'd better let well enough alone for the time being. She'd already put herself in a bad light with this man. If she intended to help Megan with her daddy she had to hold on to this job for a few more minutes, at least.

After moistening her lips with the tip of her tongue, she started again. "Your daughter wants to walk to the library with a friend. The friend's name is Cindy and she lives across the street from you. Shall I tell Megan she has your permission to go?"

Joe opened his mouth to utter a curse word, then just as quickly snapped it shut. A whole string of expletives wouldn't relieve the pressure boiling in his head. "Why does she constantly need to be going somewhere? Why can't she find something to do at home, like any normal person?"

"Because your daughter isn't any normal person. She's a teenager."

His mouth twisted. "That's supposed to explain everything?"

Savanna was struggling not to lose her patience with him. "Surely you can remember being one, can't you?"

One eyebrow arched upward as he looked at Savanna. Did he look that old to this woman?

"I'm sure the next thing you're going to tell me is that I should let her go," he said, more as a statement than a question.

What was he doing, Savanna wondered. Testing her? Was this job really being a secretary for a drilling company, or in the end would it be more about dealing with his daughter?

"Thirteen is certainly old enough to walk to the library. And it would show her you trust her to be responsible."

"I haven't been around my daughter enough to know whether I can trust her or not," he said with a pang of regret, then wondered why it had taken this woman to point that out to him. Damn it, if he'd been a better father he would have used the few weekends he'd spent with Megan to get to know her better instead of trying to entertain her.

Savanna inwardly shook her head. The man was totally serious. He'd had a daughter for thirteen years. Yet he'd just insinuated he really didn't know her. Savanna's own father was hardly perfect, but at least he'd always been there for her. But then, maybe she wasn't being entirely fair to Joe McCann, Savanna reconsidered. He might not have ever had much time with his daughter. Especially if his ex-wife hadn't wanted him in the picture.

"Well, you'll never know whether you can trust her until you give her the chance to prove herself," Savanna told him.

Joe didn't know anything about this woman except that she'd been late to work and didn't have any qualms about speaking her mind. But she had managed to pacify Megan without sticking the phone into his hand. And after several days of his daughter's endless calls, he could only see that as a major improvement.

"When she calls back, tell her she may go. But she has to be back in an hour and a half. And that you'll call the house to make sure she's returned on time."

Smiling gladly, Savanna nodded.

That settled, Joe turned and headed toward a coffee machine situated in the far corner of the room.

Bemused, Savanna asked, "Does this mean you still want me for the job?"

He glanced at her over his shoulder, and Savanna didn't miss the wry twist on his lips.

"Against my better judgment."

Chapter Two

The smile faded from Savanna's face as she folded her arms defensively over her breasts. "You really know how to make a girl feel needed, Mr. McCann."

His eyebrows peaked at her remark. It had been a long time since Joe had wanted to make anyone feel needed, he realized. Especially a woman.

"Believe me, Ms. Starr, making you feel needed was not on my agenda this morning."

Savanna's nostrils flared and Joe watched her rose-colored lips purse with disdain. He'd never particularly liked short hair on a woman. Certainly not as short as Savanna Starr's, which left her ears and neck exposed and a shock of thick blond bangs falling over her forehead. But he had to admit that it looked damn sexy on her.

"Having a flat wasn't on my agenda, either," she couldn't help retorting.

Joe glanced over at his desk. Not because he was searching for something. He merely needed to get his eyes off her and remind himself that just because she had a cute little face with warm brown eyes and a body that curved in all the right places didn't mean he needed her for a secretary. He already had enough on his mind without adding a woman to his problems.

But the way she'd dealt with Megan led him to believe she could actually help matters where his daughter was concerned. And right now that was the most important thing he needed to consider.

As though they couldn't bear it any longer, his eyes traveled back to her. "Tell me, Ms. Starr, do you normally have flat tires on your way to work? Or can I depend on you to be here on time?"

Savanna decided not to let his gibes anger her. She didn't like the wasteful emotion, and from what she could gather from the few minutes since she'd arrived, things hadn't been running very smoothly for him. She could only wonder how long it had been since he and his daughter had actually lived in the same house. And what had happened to his marriage in the first place?

Dear Lord, had she lost her mind? Joe McCann's past family life was none of her business. She shouldn't be thinking of him as a man. He was her boss! And even that was a shaky deal.

Giving herself a hard mental slap, she said, "No, I don't normally have flats and I'm rarely late."

"That's good. Because I don't need you out on Interstate 40 waiting for some macho man to come to your rescue. I need you here."

I need you. Why did those words blot out everything else he'd said up until now? Whenever she looked at him, why did she want to peel back the layers of his sarcasm and look for the real man she suspected was underneath? Changing that flat this morning must have addled her brain!

"I'll tell you what, Mr. McCann. In the future, if I need rescuing on I-40, I'll be sure to call you."

He could tell from the impish light in her eyes and the curve of her lips that she was teasing. In spite of his sour mood, he found himself wanting to smile back at her. But he didn't. He had serious things to consider. He couldn't let himself be drawn into her teasing humor.

Turning his back on her, he reached for the coffeepot. By now the liquid was burned to a bitter black, but Joe poured himself a mugful anyway. After these few minutes with Savanna he figured a shot of Scotch would have been more fitting. But since he wasn't a drinker, he'd have to rely on the caffeine to fortify him.

A few steps away, Savanna watched him swallow a mouthful of coffee, then allowed her eyes to slip down the hard-rock length of his body. He was dressed casually in blue jeans, laced-up work boots and a khaki shirt with the cuffs turned back against his forearms. He wore the clothes well, she decided. Too well for her peace of mind.

Joe took another sip of coffee, then moved back to his desk. Once there he motioned with his head for her to join him.

"Right now I think it's time we both got to work."

Her hands laced loosely in front of her, Savanna walked over and stood in front of his desk.

"I don't know how much Edie told you about the job you'll be doing here," he said, "but it's mainly answering the phone, typing correspondence and making out the payroll. Delta, our dispatcher, works in the back of the building. You'll be talking to her from time to time. Otherwise, you'll be working in this room with me."

For the first time since she'd arrived, Savanna took the time to glance around the long room. It wasn't anything fancy. Calendars, charts, maps and photographs of gas and oil wells covered most of the paneled walls. In one corner there was a small table with a coffee machine, foam cups and a bag of stale-looking doughnuts on it. Next to the table were a couple of plastic chairs. On the opposite side of the room, a few feet away from where she stood, was another metal desk and typing-style chair.

As she looked at the desk, the first thing that ran through Savanna's mind was that she'd be facing Joe McCann all day long. She couldn't imagine what that would be like. She'd worked as a temporary for several years, and during that time she'd had all sorts of bosses. But none of them had looked like Joe. Nor had they raised her hackles the way he had in the very first minute she'd met him.

Still, she wasn't about to tuck tail and run just because Joe McCann wasn't the ideal boss. She was going to stick around and make him sorry for his sarcastic attitude!

Looking at her new boss, she said, "Your secretary explained the duties of my job and how the books are set up. I'm sure I won't have any problems." Unless it's with you, she mentally added.

Joe looped his thumbs over the top of his jean pockets and continued to regard Savanna through narrowed eyes. "Edie said you've worked as a temporary for nearly five years and that you come highly recommended."

He sounded as though he found that hard to believe. Savanna decided then and there he was going to make her prove her capabilities. Well, that was all right with her. She knew how to do her job. But more than that, she knew how to adapt to new places, people and situations. She'd been doing it for as long as she could remember. And she'd do her damnedest to show he was wrong.

In spite of Joe McCann, Savanna wanted this job. She believed working for a drilling company would be interesting and helpful to the career she planned to have in accounting. Petroleum was one of the state's major industries, and gas and oil companies would always need CPAs.

True, she needed her degree in accounting before she could land a job of that importance. But Savanna only needed a few more hours of college to acquire it. And thankfully, the chance for her to complete her education had finally come to her here in Oklahoma City. She didn't intend to let anything stand in her way of that. Not even a difficult boss.

Smiling as brightly as she could manage, she said, "I've never had any complaints."

Edie had already told him that Savanna Starr was twenty-five. Yet as he looked at her smooth face and slender body, he found it hard to believe. A woman with her looks was usually married by that age. But then, maybe she was married. He hadn't asked Edie. Normally that sort of information didn't interest him and it irked the hell out of him that it did now.

"So why have you worked as a temp for so long? Wouldn't you rather have a permanent job?"

Her eyes dropped to his desktop. He'd never know just how much she wanted—needed—permanency in her life. From the time Savanna had been a small child she'd lived her life on a part-time basis. Her father's job had demanded the family move from one town and state to the next. As she'd grown older she'd planned to escape the vagabond existence as soon as she was old enough to make a permanent home for herself.

But things hadn't worked out that way. Just about the time Savanna had planned to move out, her mother had suddenly died from a stroke. After that, she knew she couldn't leave. Her father had a mild heart condition. He'd needed someone to look after him and make sure he took care of himself. Because she loved him, Savanna had stayed and never regretted it.

"Working as a temp fits my life-style. Since I've never really been sure where I was going to be living or for how long, temporary work was all I could commit myself to."

So she was a gypsy, he thought. Joe couldn't imagine such a life. He was a man who always stuck to his plan and never deviated for any reason. He couldn't imagine flitting around from one place to the next, never knowing if he'd be able to find a job or not. He worked hard to keep stability and security in his life. Yet this past month both of those things seemed to be slipping away.

Megan's arrival had definitely wrecked the stability of his day-to-day schedule. As for his drilling company, it desperately needed new revenue to stay afloat. Now, on top of everything else, he had to get used to a new secretary, one that created some strange sort of upheaval inside him every time he looked at her.

"So you move around a lot?" he asked. "You like that sort of living?"

From the expression on his face, Savanna figured he was summing her up as a flighty female who probably couldn't hang on to a job, a man or a home. The idea irked her, but she decided now wasn't the time to set him straight. She needed money for college tuition and rent for her new apartment. And this job with Joe McCann was the way to get it.

Shrugging, she said, "It's been—necessary for me to move around. But now it's not and I'm hoping to stay permanently here in Oklahoma City."

Joe shuffled a stack of papers on his desk and tried his best to appear indifferent. "Why is that? Did you marry someone here in the city?"

Surprised by his question, Savanna shook her head. "Mercy, no! I'm not looking to get married. Actually, my father remarried a couple of months ago and—well, he doesn't need me to travel with him anymore. So I'm free to sink my roots," she explained, then cast him a speculative glance. "Are you married?"

This wasn't a normal conversation between a boss and a new temporary secretary, Joe thought. He should have already pointed out her duties and gotten on with his work. But somehow one word had led to another and he still hadn't found a stopping place.

"No. I'm not. Why?"

Savanna shrugged again. "Just curious. Megan mentioned a housekeeper. I wondered if her stepmother was at work or something."

Joe heard her speaking but the words barely registered with him. He didn't know what it was about her, but she was the first woman he'd really wanted to look at in a long time. Which didn't make a bit of sense. She wasn't his type at all.

Still, he couldn't seem to stop himself from noticing the most minute things about her. Like the tiny pearl earrings she was wearing. He had the strangest urge to see what it would feel like to nibble it loose and sink his teeth into her earlobe.

Irritated by his unexpected thoughts, Joe cleared his throat and said, "No. There's no stepmother around to come between me and my daughter."

Savanna looked at him curiously. "What makes you think a stepmother would come between you and your daughter? A second mother figure might be just what she needs."

Maybe so, Joe thought, but a wife was the very last thing he needed or wanted. "And what makes you think you know so much about children? Are you a mother?" he asked.

"No. But I was a child once."

Grimacing, he picked up several pieces of correspondence. "Everyone is a child once in their life."

She was beginning to wonder if Joe McCann had ever been eight years old with freckles on his nose and a gap between his front teeth. "It's unfortunate some of us forget what that's like," she couldn't help replying.

With a warning glint in his blue eyes he thrust the papers at her. "Here's a few letters you can begin working on. I've attached notes to the things that need immediate replies. You might attend to those now."

Relieved to be out from under his scrutiny, Savanna carried the letters over to the empty desk. Before she had time to put her things away, the telephone rang. It was Megan again, who seemed very surprised when Savanna informed her that her father was allowing her to walk with her friend to the library.

"He really said I could go?"

Megan screeched the question with disbelief and Savanna could only wonder if Joe McCann was actually that strict with his daughter or if Megan was simply displaying typical teenage exaggeration. She hoped it was the latter, but from what little she'd seen of her boss this morning, she thought he probably ruled his daughter the way he ran his office. With a stern hand.

"Yes. As long as you're back in an hour and a half. I'll be calling then to make sure you're home."

"Wow, I can't wait to meet you, Savanna! Edie would never have talked Daddy into letting me go!"

Savanna glanced over at Joe, who'd now taken a seat at his desk. His attention seemed to be focused on a long piece of green graph paper with a bunch of squiggly lines that looked something like an electrocardiogram. However, Savanna got the feeling that he was actually listening to her instead of studying what she figured was a seismograph report.

"I wouldn't say that," Savanna said carefully. "It really wasn't that hard."

Megan giggled then and Savanna tried to picture the child in her mind. She sounded impish and sweet and full of life. Nothing like her father, she thought as she glanced once again at Joe McCann's bent head.

"You don't know him yet! But you will after today."

"Serious, huh?"

Megan groaned. "Look up the word in the dictionary, Savanna, and you'll find Daddy's picture beside it."

Savanna could hardly keep from laughing at the teenager's old joke, but she managed to clamp her lips together just as Joe looked up at her. "Uh, I've got to go to work, Megan."

"He's giving you one of those looks, isn't he?"

Savanna breathed deeply. Joe was giving her some sort of look. Whether it was the kind Megan meant, she didn't know. She only knew it was sending a peculiar sensation up and down her spine.

"Sorta," Savanna told her.

"Okay. Talk to you later. 'Bye!"

Savanna hung up the phone, then began searching for an empty drawer to store her purse.

"I take it that was my daughter on the phone?"

Savanna glanced over at him. "It was. She was very pleased that you're allowing her to go."

Leaning back in his chair, he regarded his new secretary with a speculative look. "The two of you seemed awfully chatty."

Savanna's brown eyes glided over his face. Was that surprise she heard in his voice, or disbelief? And why did it matter to her what he was thinking, anyway?

"I wouldn't call it chatty. Just getting acquainted."

His features suddenly growing thoughtful, Joe tapped a pen against the graph spread in front of him. "That's strange. Megan wasn't interested in getting to know Edie. In fact, they didn't get on together at all."

"Well, I'm sure you know how it is sometimes. Some people just rub each other the wrong way."

Without even knowing it, his eyes left her face to travel slowly down her body. "And how do I rub you, Ms. Starr?"

Stunned by his question, Savanna unconsciously took a step toward him. "I beg your pardon?"

What in the hell had come over him? Joe wondered wildly. He didn't talk to women that way! In fact, he didn't talk to women at all, unless it was necessary.

Clearing his throat he said, "I—that didn't come out right. What I mean is—do you think we'll be able to get along? To work together?"

From the sound of his voice, Savanna could have sworn their working together had been the last thing on his mind. But she could be wrong. After all, it would be crazy to think Joe McCann was thinking of her in that sort of way. The man didn't even appear to like her very much.

Releasing a pent-up breath, she said, "I'm a flexible person, Mr. McCann. I'm sure we can get along without too much friction between us."

"That's good," he told her with a short nod of his head. The last thing he needed between him and this delicious-looking blonde was friction of any sort.

Feeling suddenly awkward, Savanna said, "If that's all, then I'll get back to work."

Before he could say anything, the telephone rang. As he reached for it, he said, "I'll answer it this time. You go ahead and do whatever you need to do."

Relieved, Savanna went back to her desk and began organizing her things. As she did, she noticed her hands were still grimy from changing the flat tire she'd had on her way to work.

She found a rest room at the end of the same corridor she'd used to enter the office. As she scrubbed her hands clean, she looked at her image in the mirror hanging over the lavatory. There was a tiny smudge of grease along her cheekbone and she quickly wiped it away with a corner of a brown paper towel.

Maybe Joe McCann had taken the black spot for a beauty mark, Savanna thought, then laughed to herself at that idea. She doubted her new boss had even noticed the dab of grease on her face. He'd been too busy chewing her up and spitting her out for being late.

Well, he might come on like a bear, but deep down she didn't think he really was so tough. She could deal with him, Savanna promised herself. Before her job here was finished, Megan wouldn't have to beg her father to walk a few blocks to the local library and Joe McCann might even learn how to loosen up and smile.

Chapter Three

Joe's home was in a quiet, residential area that had been established years ago before the city had grown to such mammoth proportions. The house itself was red brick and situated on a large cul-de-sac. He'd lived in it with his parents from the time he was five years old. When his father died several years back, his mother had moved to Florida to retire near her sister. Since then he'd lived alone. Until last week, when Megan had moved in with him.

Tonight as he parked in the driveway and walked to the entrance, the tight ache between his shoulders reminded him how little rest he'd been getting lately. Hopefully he'd be able to eat supper and spend a quiet evening before work tomorrow.

The minute Joe stepped through the front door he was greeted with the loud blare of Megan's rock music. Tossing his briefcase full of reports into an armchair, he walked down the hallway and knocked on her door.

"Come in," Megan called loudly.

Joe pushed open the door to see his daughter lying on her stomach across the end of the bed, her elbows propped on either side of an open book.

He stepped into the room, then stared around him in disbelief. "What the he—heck has been going on in here?" Joe demanded.

Megan's head of thick brown curls bobbed wildly as she jerked her head around toward her father. "What do you mean? Nothing has been going on."

Joe went over to the stereo system and jabbed a finger on the Off button. "I'm talking about these clothes!"

Joe pointed at the countless number of garments strewn over the bed, the floor and part of the dresser.

Unconcerned, Megan pushed herself to a sitting position, then with a negligent wave of her hand she said, "Oh, I've just been trying a few things on."

A few things? It looked to him as if there were enough things on the floor alone to stock a whole boutique. "And none of them could find their way back into the closet. Is that it?" he asked.

Megan giggled at her father's grim expression. "Oh, Daddy, you're so funny. It's just clothes. They're not hurting anything. I'll pick them up before I go to bed," she promised.

Deciding it might be best to relent for now and wait to see if she kept her promise, Joe nodded toward the book she'd been so engrossed in when he'd come into the room. "Is that one of the books you got at the library today?"

She gave him a sweet smile. "Thanks, Daddy, for letting me go. The library was great! I found all sorts of stuff I want to read."

He tilted his head in an attempt to read the title printed on the spine of the book. "You didn't, uh—get anything with . . ."

"Sex, murder or corruption?" she finished for him, then, giggling, she shook her head. "No. I can get plenty of that stuff on TV."

Joe could hardly argue that point and he realized how different things were now than when he'd been Megan's age. Savanna Starr thought he didn't remember being a child, but he did.

Unlike Megan, his parents had lived together. But they'd never gotten along. Joe knew his father was a big reason for that. Joseph McCann had been a tough man, who'd liked his liquor and the expensive gamble of wildcatting. Joe could still hear his parents' shouting matches and how alone and miserable they'd made him feel.

There'd been times he'd looked at Megan and felt guilty because he hadn't been able to hold his marriage to her mother together. But now when those thoughts assaulted him, he deliberately remembered back to his own childhood, and he knew that giving Deirdre the divorce she'd wanted had been the right thing to do.

"Have you eaten yet?" he asked his daughter.

With a cheerful smile she jumped up from the bed and looped her arm through his. "Yes. But I'll come fix your plate for you. Ophelia showed me how to heat everything up in case you were late."

Out in the kitchen Megan made a big production of heating the casserole and preparing him a glass of iced tea. When everything was ready she carried it over to him on a plastic tray, then plopped down on a chair next to him.

Joe took a bite of the food, then glanced at his daughter. Her chin was in her hand and she was studying him as if she couldn't quite decide whether he was her hero or the devil himself.

"Well, how are things going?"

"I mostly miss all my friends. It's boring around here without anyone to talk to or do things with."

"You'll make plenty of friends once you start school this fall," Joe said matter-of-factly.

Megan's mouth turned down at the corners. "I doubt it. I don't want to go to some dumb ole private school. I'll have to wear some childish uniform and look like all the other nerdy girls there!"

Joe cast her a stern look of warning. "I don't want to hear you call anyone nerdy. You don't know what the girls at school will be like. You've never been there before."

She lifted her chin defiantly and glared at him with eyes as blue as his own. "And I won't go, either."

Joe shoveled another bite of food to his mouth before he lost his appetite. "You'll go if I say so."

Megan jumped up from the chair and jammed her fists on either side of her waist. "Daddy, I want to be a cheerleader and go to football games! I want to go to proms and dances. You can't do that without boys around!"

Joe put his fork down beside his plate and leaned back in his chair. He'd almost forgotten how quiet the house used to be before Megan arrived. Still, he loved her utterly, and more than anything he wanted the very best for her.

"You're far too young to be thinking about boys. Besides, school is about getting an education, not playing sports and dancing."

Megan rolled her eyes. "You're always so serious, Daddy. Don't you know a person has to have some fun once in a while?"

"Fun is knowing you've succeeded at achieving your goals."

Groaning with disbelief, Megan flounced over to the refrigerator and pulled out a can of soda. "Fun is going to the

beach or the movies. But I guess you don't do those things,"
she said sullenly.

He picked up his fork and stabbed it at the pile of noo-
dles on his plate. Hell, if he let Megan's temperament spoil
his appetite every time he sat down to supper, he'd soon turn
into a skeleton.

Megan came back to the table and sank into the same seat
she'd just vacated moments earlier. Swiping her hair out of
her eyes, she said in a perkier voice. "Your new secretary
sounds very nice. When am I going to get to meet her?"

He glanced at his daughter with surprise. "Why would
you want to meet my new secretary?"

The teenager let out another loud groan. "Because everyone around here is a stranger to me. And she sounded
like someone I'd like to know."

"How could you tell? You only talked to her on the phone
for a few short minutes," Joe observed.

"Well, I could just tell. Is she pretty?"

He choked on the tea he'd been about to swallow.
"Pretty? Why in the world would you want to know that?"

"Because if she was pretty, you might not come home in
such a cranky mood," Megan reasoned. "Is she married?"

Knowing his daughter probably wouldn't hush until he
answered, he said, "No. Ms. Starr isn't married. And yes,
she's very beautiful. But I doubt you'll have a chance to
meet her before Edie comes back to work."

Megan eyed her father over the rim of her soda can.
"What if I go to the office for a while?"

"Maybe later. I've got too much going on right now."

A grimace twisted her young face. "Then let's invite Ms.
Starr to supper. Yeah! That would be fun. Will you ask her,
Daddy? Will you?"

"No. She's a secretary. Bosses don't do that sort of thing
with their secretaries. It isn't—proper."

"Daddy, it's not like you're going to have an affair with her!"

Dear Lord, did all thirteen-year-olds talk like his? Joe wondered. "And what do you know about affairs? That word shouldn't even be in your vocabulary, yet."

Tilting her head to one side, Megan said, "Back home, my friend Amy's father had an affair. After that, her parents got a divorce. Is that what happened to you and Mom? Did you have an affair with some woman you liked better than her?"

Joe frowned at his daughter's speculation. "No, neither one of us did anything of the sort. Your mother and I were simply too young to be married. Both of us wanted totally different life-styles and because we did, we argued all the time. So we decided it would be better if we didn't live together anymore. We've told you this before. Don't you remember?"

Megan nodded, while absently winding a strand of hair around her finger. "Yeah, I remember. But I thought you might not be telling me the truth."

Joe reached out and gently touched his daughter's face. She was so young and innocent and full of life. He didn't want her ever to be hurt by anything. Especially from mistakes he'd made in the past or any he might make in the future.

"Megan, I'll never lie to you. Not about anything. Okay?"

She nodded, then gave him an impish grin. "So why haven't you gotten married again? I think you should."

A second mother figure might be just what she needs.

Joe inwardly shook his head as Savanna's voice came back to him. He'd thought the woman had been totally on the wrong track, that Megan would resent the very idea of a stepmother. Obviously he'd been wrong about Savanna and his daughter.

"And why do you think that?"

"You don't seem too happy like this."

Savanna had implied the same thing when she'd compared him to that hound with a flea on its back. But just because two females made the same conjecture about him didn't mean they were right, Joe told himself. He was happy, damn it. As happy as he could ever hope to be.

"My job gives me a lot to worry about, Megan. Believe me, the last thing I need to make me happy is a wife."

Across town Savanna carried paper plates, sodas and iced glasses to a card table set up on a small patio outside her father's apartment.

A few feet away from her, in one corner of the tiny square of yard, Thurman Starr was turning steaks on a smoking barbecue grill. Beside him, standing a good foot shorter than his six-foot frame, her new stepmother, Gloria, swiped a hand across her damp brow.

"I don't know which is cooking the most out here, us or the steaks," the older woman said.

Savanna gave her father a teasing grin, then winked at Gloria.

"I think Dad would haul that grill with him as far as the equator. When he's barbecuing, he doesn't know if the weather is ten degrees or a hundred."

Thurman laughed. "You two girls are getting soft on me. This is lovely weather. Couldn't wish for better. Besides, I have to have my grill with me. Otherwise, every piece of meat Gloria gets her hands on turns into a piece of black shoe leather."

Gloria wrinkled her nose at her husband. "Well, we'll see who cooks your breakfast in the morning," she warned playfully.

Savanna smiled to herself. It was was wonderful to see her father so happily married. At fifty, with dark brown hair and a slim, petite figure, Gloria was still youthful and pretty. But more importantly, she was a sweet, giving person. She adored Thurman and made it her job to make him feel wanted and loved.

Sadly, that hadn't been the case with Savanna's mother, Joan. She'd been a discontented woman and no matter how hard Thurman had tried to please her, she'd never seemed to be truly satisfied. Joan had always wished for things, but she'd been unwilling to bend and work to get them.

Savanna had grown up vowing not to make the same mistakes her mother had. Whatever she decided she wanted in life, she was going to go after it full force. If she had to deviate from her plan at times, she would. But she'd never give up her dreams.

And she hadn't given up that vow to be happy, Savanna thought as she placed silverware beside the three plates. But she'd certainly learned the hard way that determination alone wasn't quite enough to make all her dreams come true.

In her senior year of high school she'd fallen in love and had become engaged to be married shortly after graduation. But only days before the wedding Bruce had left town with another girl.

The betrayal had angered and humiliated Savanna, but she'd resolved not to let it sour her outlook on love and marriage. By the time she'd entered college the following fall, her heart had mended and before long she'd met a young man in one of her accounting classes. Terry had been charming and had seemed to genuinely love her. After a few months of dating Savanna had been certain that she'd found her true soul mate this time. They'd become engaged and had begun to plan their life together. But fate had stepped in once again and Terry had been killed in a car accident a month before their wedding day.

Savanna had been devastated. Not only had she lost the man she loved, but Terry's death had made her look at life with new eyes. And it was clear to her that marriage and a family wasn't supposed to be a part of her life.

Then a month later her mother had died. And suddenly love and marriage didn't matter to Savanna anymore. Her father was grieving, she was grieving and they needed each other.

That had been five years ago, and even though she'd put all the pain and loss of that time behind her, Savanna wasn't ready to put marriage back into her hopes and dreams. She'd learned that loving a man and having him love her back didn't make for any sort of guarantees. One day she'd been deliriously happy, the next her whole world had shattered.

No, Savanna firmly told herself, unlike her mother she was going to be happy. Only now she was going to find happiness in something more predictable than love and marriage.

A few minutes later the steaks were done and the table set. As the three of them filled their plates Thurman asked his daughter, "How was your first day on the job, honey? Think you're gonna like it?"

Reaching for her glass of soda, Savanna groaned, albeit good-naturedly. "I don't know whether like is the right word. Maybe you should have asked if I was going to be able to endure it."

Gloria looked at her stepdaughter with concern. "Was it that bad? I was hoping this was going to be an interesting job for you."

Savanna shrugged as Joe McCann's face floated in front of her eyes. "Well, I suppose you could call it interesting. Tense, but interesting."

"What about your new boss, is he a nice man?" Gloria questioned.

Unconsciously Savanna drew in a deep breath then let it out slowly. Throughout the day she hadn't been able to forget that her boss was sitting only a few feet away from her. Every few minutes she'd found herself forgetting her work and glancing over at him.

To make matters worse, each time Savanna had looked, Joe McCann had lifted his head and their eyes had clashed. Exchanging glances with the man had been unsettling, to say the least. It was as if arcs of electricity had passed between them and she didn't know why. Her boss hadn't so much as given her a smile!

Yet she'd been home for several hours and still couldn't get her mind off him. It was crazy! A part of her dreaded the morning and seeing him again, while the other part was eager to be back in his company.

Savanna grimaced. "If he's nice, he keeps it well hidden. At best, I'd describe him as sober."

"Look, baby," her father said as he sliced into the juicy beef, "if the man is that bad, you don't have to work for him. I can give you enough money to tide you over until you find something better."

Savanna had stopped taking financial help from her father a long time ago, but he never ceased offering, anyway.

"Thanks, Dad," she told Thurman, "but I have no intentions of quitting. In fact, the drilling business is far more interesting than I thought it would be. So far today, I've learned it takes all sorts of people to drill for gas or oil. Geologist, seismologist, construction crews, truck drivers, drillers, tool pushers, rigworkers, roustabout crews and especially some rich financier to back it all. I think it will be a good learning experience to find out just what these people do to get petroleum out of the ground.''

"Well, perhaps your boss simply had a bad day. It might be that tomorrow he'll loosen up and you'll be able to enjoy your job," Gloria put in hopefully.

Joe McCann loosen up? Savanna had held hopes for that this morning. But after spending a whole day with him? Well, she was still trying to figure out just exactly what it would take to put a smile on the man's face.

"I don't know, Gloria," Savanna said doubtfully. "I have a feeling *every* day is a bad day for Mr. McCann."

Across the table Thurman chuckled. "If anybody can loosen him up, it'll be you, Savanna. He'll think a hurricane has hit his office before you get through with him."

Savanna laughed along with her father. She might as well. It was too late to fret now. She'd stayed at McCann's this morning in spite of the shaky start she'd gotten off to with her stern-faced boss, and in doing so, she'd committed herself to the job. Savanna had never backed out of a commitment for any reason and she wasn't about to now. She only hoped Joe McCann didn't make her regret it.

Chapter Four

McCann Drilling was located on the west edge of Oklahoma City and several miles from Savanna's apartment.

The next morning Savanna made doubly sure she had plenty of time to drive to work and, if necessary, change a flat. In fact, she got to McCann's so early she discovered the door to the office building still locked and Joe nowhere in sight.

Deciding she didn't want to sit in her Volkswagen until he arrived, she climbed out of the car and walked over to a high chain-link fence. It started at one end of the office building and stretched far into the distance. Behind the fence, more than a hundred yards away, several men were already at work loading a mammoth piece of iron derrick onto a long flatbed trailer.

The work yard appeared to cover at least five acres of land. Savanna knew practically nothing about the petroleum industry, yet in spite of her ignorance, one thing stood out loud and clear. McCann Drilling wasn't busy.

A long line of blue-and-white transport trucks were sitting idle, mountains of drilling pipe lay stacked on its sides, while pieces of derrick were piled end upon end of each other, lying in useless wait. The rows of huge motors, which she guessed were used as power to turn the drilling pipe as it worked its way into the ground, were all quiet. How long had it been this way? she wondered.

"I see you made it safely to work on time this morning, Ms. Starr."

At the sound of Joe's voice, she turned away from the link fence to see him walking down the sidewalk toward her. As her eyes drank in the sight of him, her heart began to thud like a bass drum.

He was dressed all in blue denim this morning. The jeans were obviously worn and faded to a lighter shade than the shirt and clung to his long, muscled legs like an old familiar glove. Like yesterday, the sleeves on his shirt were rolled back against his forearms. A thin gold watch circled his left wrist, but other than that he wore no jewelry.

Savanna had never worked for a man who dressed as if he were part cowboy. But then, she'd never really lived in the Midwest before, either. Maybe the men here were different. Or maybe Joe McCann had his own ideas about business clothes. Whatever the reason, she found it very hard not to think of him as a man, when every inch of him looked tough and masculine. Right down to the laced boots on his feet.

Once he finally reached her, she smiled and said, "Fortunately, I didn't have a breakdown this morning."

"That's good. I didn't want to have to go after you in one of the gin trucks."

Was he actually teasing her? Savanna quickly studied his face, then felt strangely disappointed when she found nothing there. Not even the merest hint of a smile.

"I'm afraid I'm going to have to plead my ignorance. I don't know what a gin truck is."

Joe pointed to a truck the workmen were using to hoist up a piece of derrick. "The one that looks like a big wrecker."

She nodded that she understood, then glanced back over to him. "I've been standing here trying to figure out what most of this stuff is," she said, waving her hand out toward the work yard. "You have so much of everything. McCann Drilling must be a big operation."

The corners of his mouth twisted wryly. "It's not Exxon or Texaco by any means."

"Lucky for you."

Frowning, he looked at her. "What do you mean, lucky for me?"

She laughed at his nonplussed expression and Joe was struck by the freshness of her face, the vibrancy of her voice. She was wearing a sundress printed with large black-eyed Susans. It had a full skirt and two little straps over each shoulder. It wasn't a dress he considered fitting for a secretary, but on Savanna he had to admit that somehow it managed to look sexy and charming at the same time.

"I meant it would be terrible to be saddled with something that big," she told him.

He grunted as though her remark was addlebrained. "Every oilman dreams of making it big someday."

Since Savanna had moved to this city, the wind had never ceased to blow. Now she watched it tug strands of Joe's tawny blond hair across his forehead. "Are you an oilman, Mr. McCann?"

Obviously from the droll look on his face, he thought Savanna's question a waste of time. "That is what I do, Ms. Starr. I search for oil or gas."

"But is that what you really strive for, to make it big in the business? Do you want to be able to look up some day and say I'm the new king of the American road?"

From the moment Joe had met this woman yesterday morning she'd put him to thinking about things he'd never stopped to examine that closely before. First his daughter and now his work. What was it about her, anyway? Was she trying to practice psychology on the side and using him for a new patient?

"As far as I'm concerned I don't think Texaco has anything to worry about. Hell, just look out there, Ms. Starr. You see all those stacked out-rigs? That's not a work yard anymore, it's a damn graveyard."

She followed the line of his vision. "Well, I do know that the price of raw crude is down now. I guess your work is constantly affected by supply and demand."

He grimaced as he continued to watch the skeleton crew of men at work. "You're right, Ms. Starr. And this past year demand has been at rock bottom."

So business had been bad for a whole year, Savanna concluded. Was that the reason he'd forgotten how to smile? The question made her look at him and wonder what kind of man he'd been before business had gone downhill. Was it possible that he'd actually been a happy, carefree man back then, or had something other than his business stepped in to change him? A woman? His daughter?

Savanna, stop wondering about your boss, she silently scolded herself. It shouldn't make any difference to her if the man used to be a stand-up comedian. He was simply her boss and a few weeks from now, when her job for him had come to an end, he'd merely be a man she used to work for.

But it did matter, a part of her argued. She could see dark clouds of weariness in his eyes and the sight of it saddened her. She knew what it was like to wake up each morning and feel as if a dreadful weight was hanging around her neck. She wanted to help him. She wanted to see him laugh. She wanted him to be able to face whatever problems he had to face with a light heart and a hopeful smile.

"Things will pick up," she said with bright encouragement.

"I've been telling myself that for a long time now."

She turned away from the fence to look at him squarely. "Well, you know how the old saying goes. You can get a good man down, but you can't keep him there."

Turning, Joe folded his arms across his chest and stared down at her like an infuriated drill sergeant at a green recruit.

"My father was the good man, Ms. Starr. When he was alive and running the company, this place was going twenty-four hours a day. We couldn't drill fast enough. He knew where to find revenue, he knew how to convince people to drill another hole when there were already two dry holes in the same section of land. People believed in him and were willing to take a gamble."

Savanna didn't know why he seemed so angry about it all. She'd only been trying to make him feel better. But apparently he didn't want to do anything but growl.

"And people don't believe you're capable of finding crude?" she came back. "Well, Mr. McCann, have you ever asked yourself if you're in the wrong business?"

She wouldn't have thought it possible, but his face seemed to grow even harder. "I think what you should do, Ms. Starr, is mind your own business."

Resisting the urge to grind her teeth, she drew up her shoulders and brushed past him. "Fine. If you'll be kind enough to open the office door, I'll get to work minding my own business."

Suddenly bemused by her quick change in temperament, Joe turned and watched her retrieve her purse and lunch bag from the passenger seat of the orange Volkswagen. As she walked to the front entrance of the office building, her black high heels clicked angrily on the sidewalk. At that moment everything about him, his father and the business fled his mind. All he could think about was the wind catching the hem of her dress and lifting it away from her legs. They were gorgeous. He'd noticed that at least a hundred times yesterday when she'd had on that skimpy little yellow thing. It was only normal male instinct that he wanted to see them again.

Too bad her mouth wasn't as gorgeous as her legs, he thought irritably as he pulled a ring of keys from his jeans pocket and started toward her. Hell, Joe, her mouth is as luscious looking as everything else on her, a little voice inside him pointed out, you just don't like the words that come out of it. And apparently she didn't like what came out of his.

Well, that was all right with Joe. As long as the two of them disliked each other, he wouldn't be tempted to think of her as a woman. Still, he couldn't help but wonder what it would be like to kiss that mouth of hers shut.

Moments later Joe had the plate-glass door open. Savanna hurried in ahead of him, then quickly realized she had to wait for him to open the door leading directly into the office.

Standing to one side of the narrow corridor, she watched him flip through his key ring. "When does the mail arrive?" she asked coolly.

"Soon."

Savanna impatiently tapped the toe of her high heel and prayed for him to hurry. She didn't like being this close to him. Everything about him, from the crisp scent of his aftershave to the tawny blond hair covering his forearms to the broad width of his shoulders, made her feel like a woman. More of a woman than she'd ever felt in her life. And the realization shook her.

Joe finally found the correct key, yet before he jabbed it into the lock he paused and looked over at Savanna. "By the way," he said, "my daughter likes you."

His words took her by surprise. Unconsciously her lips parted as she met his gaze. "Oh?"

She was wearing red lipstick today and little black drops in her ears that jiggled each time she moved her head. Until Savanna had whirled into his life yesterday morning he'd never met a woman that made him aware of every little thing about her. But she did. She made a mess of his thinking. In fact, when he looked at her, he found it difficult to think at all.

"Yeah. She says she'd like to get to know you."

He said it as if he found it incredible that anyone could actually like her. Savanna bristled like a cornered cat. "Well, it's obvious she has different taste than her father."

A crooked grin suddenly spread across his face. The sight of it was so transforming and so shocking she drew in a sharp breath that hissed between her teeth.

"Why, Ms. Starr, I do believe you have a temper."

Instantly Savanna decided it didn't matter what he'd said to her. The man could smile. Somewhere buried inside him there had to be a bit of humor. If she did anything while she was here at McCann Drilling, she was going to find it.

"For your information, I have to be very provoked to lose my temper." She didn't go on to tell him he'd already done a good job of rousing her ire.

"So you're telling me you normally have a sweet, placid temper?"

She gave him an impish smile. "Can't you tell?"

With a wry shake of his head, Joe stuck the key in the lock and pushed open the door. She swished past him and just for a moment, as her sweet scent drifted to his nostrils, he had the insane urge to grab her arm and tug her up against him. He wanted to kiss her. He wanted to see those snappy brown eyes of hers go all soft and sexy.

Thank God he caught himself just in time. The last thing he needed to be doing was kissing Savanna Starr. He had a drowning drilling business to take care of and a daughter who desperately needed guidance. Sex wasn't on his agenda, even with a woman who looked as delicious as Savanna.

Inside the office Joe quickly put fresh coffee makings together. By the time it had brewed the mail arrived. While he was going through the stack of envelopes, Savanna posted a few transactions in the bookkeeping ledger. Once she was finished with that job, she poured herself a cup of coffee and waited for him to give her the correspondence that needed immediate answers.

"I suppose I should apologize to you," she said as she stood looking out a window and sipping her coffee.

Her unexpected statement had Joe lifting his head to look across the room at her. "Apologize for what?"

She kept her eyes on the work yard. "Well, I obviously insulted you this morning when I suggested you should do something other than drilling for gas or oil. You were right, it wasn't any of my business."

"Forget it," he said brusquely, then turned his attention back to the letter he was reading.

Savanna moved away from the window and over to his desk. "You said your father used to run this business. Has it been long since he passed away?"

Joe glanced back up to see her standing at the corner of his desk, her small hands wrapped around a coffee cup, her face a picture of quiet beauty.

"Seven years. He collapsed on a drilling site down in eastern Oklahoma. By the time we could get him into a hospital he'd died from a bleeding ulcer."

Savanna shook her head. It was impossible for her to imagine the horror Joe must have felt as he helplessly watched his father die. "What a terrible thing."

Joe shrugged as though he'd long ago accepted his father's death. "Some rigs might be ten, even fifteen miles back into the rough mountains. It takes a while to make a trip in or out. And," he went on with a heavy sigh, "Dad liked his Kentucky bourbon as much as he liked seeing a drill pipe sink into the earth. Alcohol tends to destroy the stomach's lining. He knew that."

"I can't imagine losing my father," she said thoughtfully. "He's a wonderful man. Very smart and equally charming. He just married a woman from here in the city. I'm going to miss them both when they leave."

Joe didn't have time for this sort of visiting. He couldn't remember the last time he'd simply sat and talked to someone other than his daughter or a potential client. But to his surprise he didn't want to tell Savanna to go back to work and leave him alone. When she was around him he thought about her instead of Megan and how he was going to convince her to enroll in private school. Hell, he even forgot that McCann Drilling was about one step away from bankruptcy.

"Your father and stepmother are planning to move?"

A wistful smile on her face, she nodded. "Oh, yes. You see, my dad's job is setting up businesses with their own computer systems, then teaching the employees how to use them. Once that's accomplished, he moves on to the next place. Up until a few months ago I always packed up and moved with him. But now he has Gloria and doesn't need me to live with him."

"Why did he need you to live with him?" Joe couldn't help asking.

"Oh, well, to hear Daddy tell it, he didn't need me to live with him these past five years since my mother's death. He'll tell you I was just reluctant to leave the nest," she said with a fond smile. "But actually, Daddy has a mild heart condition and I wanted to be near him to make sure he took care of himself and that if he did become ill, I'd be there to help him."

Yesterday he'd privately labeled Savanna a gypsy and figured she'd worked as a temporary because she wasn't capable of holding down a permanent job. Now Joe had to admit that he couldn't have been more wrong about her. She wasn't a vagabond, she was a devoted daughter.

Joe shook his head. "Five years is a long time to be your father's caretaker. Most women your age have already gotten married and had children."

The last he said more as a question than a statement, and that surprised Savanna. She couldn't imagine that he might actually be interested in her personal life.

"Not all women want to get married. Some of us have other plans for our lives," she told him, then suddenly his probing eyes became too much for her to bear. Focusing her gaze on the toes of her black pumps, she added, "Actually, I don't think marriage is in the cards for me."

Joe started to ask her why, but the wistful shadow on her face stopped him. Something had happened to her in the past and he instinctively knew he was better off not knowing about it. He needed to keep out of her personal life completely. She'd already taken up too much of his thoughts and his time.

When it appeared her boss wasn't going to say anything else, Savanna went over to her own desk and sat down. She needed something to do, anything to keep her busy and her mind off Joe. But he obviously wasn't finished with the mail and the phone hadn't yet rung once. He hadn't been exaggerating when he'd said this place was more like a graveyard than a drilling company.

Restlessly Savanna fiddled with a notepad lying next to her typewriter. Then suddenly, as if she were sending desperate telepathic messages, the telephone shrilled.

"McCann Drilling," she answered as quickly as she could snatch up the receiver.

"Hi, Savanna! It's me, Megan."

Savanna smiled at the sound of the young girl's voice. "Oh, hi, Megan. How are you this morning?"

"I'm okay, I guess. Are you busy?"

From the corner of her eye she could see Joe was watching her. Trying her best to ignore him, she said, "Not at the moment. Did you need something?"

"Not really," Megan said gloomily. "I just wanted to talk. It gets pretty lonely around here."

Savanna's heart went out to her. "I'm sure it does. I used to have to move with my parents a lot. It's a bummer at first, but after a while things get better. You'll meet new friends."

Megan groaned. "I won't ever meet anybody sitting here in this house, and Daddy never does anything but work."

Savanna wasn't surprised to hear this. Joe hardly seemed the socializer type. "Well, school will be starting in a couple of months. Things will change for you then."

"Ugh, don't mention school," Megan wailed. "Daddy has all sorts of weird ideas about that. But that's not what I really wanted to talk to you about. Do you think you could come over to our house Friday night for supper?"

Savanna hardly knew what to say. Even though she didn't really know Megan, the needy sound of her voice tugged at Savanna's heart. She would like nothing more than to befriend the girl. But how could she? Joe hadn't invited her and she doubted he knew what his daughter was up to.

Unconsciously, she flipped the corners of the notepad with her fingernail as she searched for the kindest way out of this. "Megan, that might not—uh, go over very well with your father."

"It'll be all right, Savanna," the teenager quickly assured her. "I told him last night that I want you to come."

So why hadn't he already suggested it to her? Savanna wondered. Glancing across at him, she saw that he was studying her openly, as though he were waiting for her to hand him a major problem. And that annoyed her. Did the man have to always look on the pessimistic side? "Just a minute, Megan."

Placing a hand over the receiver, she said to Joe, "Megan has invited me to your house for supper Friday."

His blue eyes flew wide open. "She what!"

"I said—"

"I know what you said," he snapped angrily. "I want to know what she thinks she's doing."

Savanna silently counted to ten. "It's pretty obvious to me. She's reaching out to make a friend."

Joe snorted. "She has friends. There's no need for her to go behind my back and issue an invitation I didn't okay first."

Suddenly it didn't matter if Joe McCann fired her or not—he needed to have his eyes opened. About his daughter and a whole lot of other things.

Removing her hand from the mouthpiece, she said, "Megan, wait just a minute. I've got to put you on hold."

Once the button on the telephone was pushed, Savanna got up from her seat and walked over to his desk. Joe's face was a picture of astonishment as she placed her palms upon the polished oak and leaned toward him.

"Do you consider your home your daughter's home, too?" she asked.

Her voice was a bit too calm and sweet for Joe's liking. He frowned at her. "Of course, but—"

"Oh, I see. It's her home, but she isn't allowed to invite anyone to visit her there. Is that right?"

"No. That isn't right. But she has to use discretion—"

The hiss of Savanna's sharply indrawn breath halted his words. He'd thought she'd been angry yesterday morning, but the sparks flying from her brown eyes told him he hadn't yet seen her true temper. But Joe had the feeling he was about to.

"In other words, she can't go around inviting scum like me to your house. Well, for your information, Mr. McCann, I—"

"That's not what I meant!" Joe practically shouted the interruption.

Her face inched closer to his. "You don't lie very well, Mr. McCann."

Right at the moment he wasn't doing anything very well, he thought. He wasn't quite sure how he'd gotten himself into such a spot. Moreover, he didn't know how he was going to get himself out of it without insulting his new secretary any more than he already had.

"You're calling me a liar now?"

Savanna didn't back away from him, even though he was looking at her as though he'd like nothing better than to put his hand around her throat and choke the life out of her. "If the shoe fits," she quipped.

His nostrils flared as he drew in a deep breath. "My daughter is none of your business."

"It's pretty obvious she isn't yours, either."

Joe jumped to his feet. Savanna straightened, then rose on her tiptoes to better look him in the eye.

"Just what are you implying, Ms. Starr?"

Knowing she'd gone too far to stop now, Savanna jammed her hands at either side of her waist and said, "I'm implying that when daddy lessons were given you must have been absent for the whole course!"

"And just what makes you an authority on fathering? Hell, you're not a man. You're not even a mother!"

He was back in his drill-sergeant mode. His arms were folded against his chest, his jaw set like a rock and his eyes were two blue blazes of fury. Savanna wanted to hit him where he needed it the most. Right in the mouth.

"No. But I was a teenaged girl once, just like Megan. And I know what it feels like to be in a strange city without her friends or anyone to talk to."

"And just what am I?" he retorted.

Savanna's lips twisted mockingly. "You don't really want me to answer that, Mr. McCann."

Joe's eyes slid over her flushed face, then lower to where her bosom heaved against the black-eyed Susans. He didn't know what it was about her that got to him. Even when she was angry and impertinent and saying things to him that no other woman had ever dared say, he wanted to kiss her. She was like a beautiful little wildcat that he desperately wanted to tame.

"Even though you probably don't believe it, Ms. Starr, I do love my daughter and I'm trying to be sensitive to her needs."

"You're right. I'm finding it very hard to believe," she said, then with a huge sigh she shook her head. "Look, I know you don't really know me that well. And I understand that you don't want me invading the privacy of your home. I won't do that. I'll take Megan somewhere for pizza and we can have a nice girl chat on our own. She's still waiting on the line, so what do you say?"

What was the matter with him? Joe wondered. He knew that Savanna wasn't going to be a bad influence on his daughter. As far as that went, he figured she could even be a help where Megan was concerned. But Joe was reluctant to let her into their home and into his daughter's life. Because he knew that once he did, she would be in his life, too.

Joe was already wildly attracted to the woman. It would be inviting trouble to spend any more time with her than necessary. Still, Joe loved his daughter and if Savanna was the key to putting a little happiness in her life, then he couldn't bring himself to stand in the way.

His features impassive, he reached for the telephone and handed the receiver to Megan. "Tell her you'll be at our house for supper."

Savanna's brows lifted with surprise as she took the instrument from him. "What about us going out for pizza?"

Suddenly finding it hard to keep looking her in the eye, Joe glanced down at his desktop and quickly snatched up his coffee cup. "I don't really want her eating in fast-food joints. And Ophelia always makes extra for the evening meal."

Savanna couldn't believe he'd caved in about the whole thing. Especially when he obviously didn't want her to be in his home. But she was glad. Like Megan, she was new to this city. She needed friends, too.

Quickly she punched a button on the phone to open the line. "Megan? Sorry I had to keep you waiting for so long. Your father and I had a few things to discuss."

"Yeah, I'll bet. He's big on discussions."

The teenager said it so matter-of-factly that Savanna wanted to laugh. "Yes. Well, we've gotten it all over with and I wanted to tell you that I'm looking forward to seeing you Friday night for supper."

There was a pause and then Megan's young voice squealed with surprise. "You will? Really? Wow! That's great, Savanna! I can't wait to meet you. I know you're gonna be really beautiful."

A puzzled frown on her face, Savanna asked, "What in the world makes you say that?"

Megan giggled. "Because Daddy already told me so. 'Bye, Savanna! See you Friday!"

With slow, thoughtful movements Savanna replaced the receiver on the hook, then glanced across the room to where Joe was pouring himself a second cup of coffee.

Did Joe McCann really think she was beautiful? The mere idea left her trembling. Savanna couldn't imagine him saying such a thing to his daughter, much less thinking it.

But what if he had been looking at her in a purely male way? What if he was attracted to her?

None of that mattered, she firmly told herself. She didn't want a man in her life. Not on a short-term basis. Not permanently. Not any way. Savanna's heart was still covered with scars of grief. She wasn't about to risk having it broken all over again by a man like Joe McCann.

The man had forgotten how to smile. She might be able to teach him how to do that again. But she doubted any woman could teach him how to love. And Savanna certainly wasn't about to try.

"If you ask me, this is all very strange," Jenny said as she watched Savanna push clothes back and forth on the closet rod.

Savanna looked over at her friend, who had draped herself across the end of the bed. She'd met the redhead two months ago when she'd moved into the apartment directly across from hers. Jenny was in her thirties and had worked as a city policewoman for several years. The stressful job had broken her marriage and left her a bit jaded about men in general. But she had a wonderful sense of humor and Savanna had been drawn to her from the very first moment they'd met.

"There's nothing strange about it," Savanna assured her.

"Last night you told me your boss was stiff and stern and made you very uncomfortable. Now you're saying you're going to have dinner with the man. If that makes sense I'd better start looking for a therapist. I'm in worse shape than I thought."

Laughing, Savanna pulled a red cotton dress from the closet, then held it out in front of her for a better look. "You don't need a therapist to tell you you're crazy. I can do that for free."

Jenny shot her a dry look. "Thanks, Savanna. Now that I've got you for a free therapist, do you know any plastic surgeons that live in the building? I might manage to get a free eye job."

Savanna made a face at her. "Your eyes are beautiful and as for Joe McCann, I'm not really having dinner with him. I'm going to meet his daughter."

"The man is married?" Jenny asked with surprise.

Savanna tossed the red dress onto the bed. "No. He has a daughter from an earlier marriage. How that ended, I don't know. But Megan has recently come to live with him and she's feeling pretty lost and alone since moving away from her friends."

Jenny picked up the dress, then shook her head. "Not this one, honey. Why don't you wear that perky little split-skirt thing? The brown one trimmed with stripes."

Savanna glanced doubtfully at her friend, then back to the closet. "You think so? I don't know. It's so short. It only comes to the middle of my thighs."

The redhead rolled her eyes. "Savanna, if I were twenty-five again and had legs like yours, I'd be showing them off all the time."

With a hopeless shake of her head, Savanna put the red dress back in the closet and searched for the brown one. "Jenny, I'm not going over to the McCanns to impress my boss. And even if I was, I certainly wouldn't do it with my legs."

Jenny burst out laughing. "So how would you impress this cool Joe McCann, if you had a mind to, that is?"

Savanna tossed the brown dress onto the bed, then walked over to the dresser and picked up a hairbrush. "I don't know. I can't really figure the man. He's strictly business."

"Oh, I see. I'll bet he's one of those skinny, balding, thick-lensed glasses types who has more money than he has brains. Just like the guy I work with now. Ugh! The man isn't safe with a gun on his hip!"

Frowning, Savanna pulled the brush through her hair. "Well, thankfully Joe isn't anything like that. He looks as stout as a bull and he doesn't wear glasses."

"What color are his eyes?"

"Sky blue," Savanna answered automatically, then turned on her friend with a sly laugh. "All right. That's enough. I know exactly what you're doing and before you go any farther, let me tell you that even though Joe Mc-Cann is a handsome man, I'm not interested."

The look Jenny gave her was pointed and full of humor. "No, you're only interested in his daughter."

"That's right," Savanna said as she ruffled her fingers through her short blond hair. "Megan is thirteen. She needs a friend and she also needs help with her daddy."

"Why? What's wrong with the man, other than being a handsome stuffed shirt?"

Savanna made an impatient gesture with her hand. "Jenny, the man knows next to nothing about fathering."

Jenny's eyes widened. "And you're going to teach him?"

"Well, someone has to," Savanna insisted.

Shaking her head, Jenny laughed softly, then raised her eyebrows at the champagne-colored lingerie Savanna tossed onto the bed.

"Uh-huh, I can see you're definitely going to have an interesting evening," the older woman said.

"Hmph, Joe McCann will never get that close to me," Savanna said with confidence.

Jenny laughed again. "Never say never, honey."

Chapter Five

Savanna was late. Again. Pulling over to the side of the street, she carefully studied the city map. She'd never been in this part of town before and she was surprised to see that Joe lived in such a high-toned residential area. He seemed more like the ranch-house-in-the-suburbs type, but then he wasn't your everyday typical man, either.

Savanna pushed her sunglasses back up on her damp nose and shoved the map back into the glove box. It looked as though she was finally on the right street. Hopefully, two more blocks would put her at the right house.

Pulling the car away from the curb, she continued on down the street. As she drove, she couldn't help but notice the massive brick houses on either side of her were all quiet. No children were playing in the front yards. And definitely no orange Beetles sat parked in the driveways. These people drove cars with trunks bigger than her whole vehicle and air conditioners cold enough to turn a person's knees blue.

Well, Savanna's little car had an air conditioner, too, she thought humorously—two windows to roll down. But that didn't bother her. Savanna's family had never been rich. Comfortable, but not rich. And Savanna herself had never been impressed with money or things. She cared more about the inside of a person, not the outside trappings.

A minute later she circled a cul-de-sac and spotted the pickup truck Joe drove to work. With a sigh of relief she stopped her little car behind it, quickly powdered her face, then dashed up the steps to the front entrance.

Before Savanna had a chance to ring the bell, the door jerked open and a tall young girl with a head full of brown curls stood smiling back at her.

"Hi, Savanna! We've been waiting on you!"

She eagerly grabbed Savanna's hand and tugged her into a large foyer.

"It's nice to meet you, too, Megan," Savanna said with a laugh, then glanced up to see Joe watching the two of them from an arched doorway. As her eyes met his, her heart began to race like a deer in flight.

"Late again, Ms. Starr. What happened, did you have another flat?"

He was teasing. Savanna didn't know how she knew it. Especially when there wasn't the merest hint of a smile on his face. But she did know it and the fact left her feeling warm and just a little sassy.

"Not this time, Mr. McCann. Why, were you getting impatient for my company?"

A quirk of amusement touched his lips as his blue eyes swept down her face, then lower to the short little dress hugging her figure. "No. My supper," he said.

As Savanna looked back at him, she decided there was a hungry look in his eyes, but she had to wonder if it was solely for food.

Don't be ridiculous. She instantly scolded herself for thinking such foolishness. From his attitude so far, Joe McCann didn't particularly like her, much less find her desirable.

With that reassuring thought, she gave him a little smile and said, "Sorry. It was never my intention to keep a hungry man waiting."

Joe didn't smile back at her, but the glint in his blue eyes told Savanna he was close to it.

Clearing his throat, he said, "Ophelia has everything ready and waiting. Or would you rather have a drink before we have our supper?"

"A drink isn't necessary," Savanna assured him. "I'm ready to eat whenever you two are."

"Then we'll go on into the dining room."

With one hand he motioned for her and Megan to precede him out of the foyer and down three wide carpeted steps. They immediately entered a long living room furnished with a couple of chesterfields done in burgundy-colored leather and two hunter green armchairs, along with a deacon's bench and several more pieces of furniture. Heavy drapes were pulled across a wide expanse of windows, shutting out the waning sunset.

At one end of the room a massive stone fireplace with a slightly elevated hearth took up a major part of the wall; at the opposite end was an arched opening that led into the dining room.

As the three of them approached it, Savanna could see a long cherry-wood table set for three. Just beyond it, a bay window with a cushioned seat looked out over a large flower garden.

"This is lovely," Savanna said as Joe helped her into her chair.

"I'm glad you like it, Ms. Starr."

He took the seat just to the right of her at the head of the table. Megan took the seat directly across from her. Feeling the young girl's gaze traveling curiously over her, she looked across at Megan and gave her a smile.

"Thank you for inviting me, Megan. It was very nice of you."

The teenager's face glowed with excitement. "I'm really glad you're here, Savanna. I was afraid you might not come."

"Oh? Why did you think that?"

Megan darted a brave glance at her father, then grinned at Savanna. "Well, I was afraid Daddy might try to talk you out of it. You see, he's not the sociable type."

"Megan!" Joe warned in a low voice.

Laughter spilled from Savanna, filling the room with the tinkling sound.

Joe looked at Savanna with an annoyed frown. "Don't encourage her."

Savanna curbed her laughter, but a smile remained on her face. "Your daughter was simply stating the obvious, Mr. McCann," she told Joe, then glanced across the table at Megan, who appeared to be watching the two adults with obvious interest. "Your father was gracious enough to make an exception tonight, Megan. You should thank him for that."

"Oh, I do!" she exclaimed, then turned a sweet smile on Joe. "Thank you, Daddy, for letting me have a dinner guest tonight."

Put like that Joe couldn't remain annoyed with either of them. And suddenly he wondered what it would be like living with two precocious females instead of just one. He was a man who valued his privacy. Even his mother, whom he'd always felt relatively close to, called him a loner. Yet he found himself wondering how it would be to have Savanna's laughter continually filling this house? To always have her lovely face across from him at the supper table?

The questions came out of nowhere and for a moment Joe was addled with surprise. Since he and Deirdre had divorced, he'd never imagined any woman living in this house with him. He didn't know why Savanna was putting such family-type notions into his head. But one thing he knew for sure, he had to stop it. Megan was all the family he wanted or needed.

"You're welcome, Megan," he said to his daughter. "Now shall we eat?"

"Yes! I'm starved!" She picked up a large salad bowl filled with fresh greens and passed it to Savanna. "You first, Savanna. You're the guest."

As Savanna filled her salad plate and sprinkled it with oil and vinegar Megan asked, "Have you ever eaten catfish fillets, Savanna? That's what we're having tonight."

"No. I don't believe I have. I've eaten trout and baked salmon, but not catfish."

"Ooh, then you're in for a treat," Megan told her. "This is fried crispy."

Savanna laughed. "I've discovered that a big part of the food in this area is fried."

"Where did you last live, Ms. Starr?"

She passed the salad bowl over to Joe. As he took it from her, their eyes clashed and for a brief moment Savanna's breath hung in her throat.

"Seattle, Washington," she answered quickly. "A large insurance company needed to update their computer system, so my dad was busy there for several months before we had to move."

"It must have been quite a switch for you to come from such a cool, rainy climate to Oklahoma's blistering heat," he said as he took a portion of salad from the bowl.

"Actually, I'm enjoying it. You can't imagine how tiresome the fog and rain can be after a while."

"Did you have a boyfriend there, Savanna?" Megan asked, her eyes shining with curiosity.

"Megan! That isn't something you should be asking Ms. Starr," Joe scolded.

From the corner of her eye Savanna could see Joe's lips stretch to a thin line of disapproval and when he spoke again it was with the same growl Savanna had first heard yesterday outside his office door.

"Ms. Starr's personal life is none of our business," he added.

Seemingly undaunted by her father's rough voice, Megan giggled as she stabbed several pieces of lettuce onto her fork. "Daddy, why do you call Savanna Ms. Starr? That sounds so...unfriendly."

"It's not unfriendly. It's respectful," Joe corrected his daughter.

"Sure, if you'd only just met her. But you know her now. Why don't you call her Savanna? And Savanna, why don't you call Daddy Joe? That sounds much nicer than mister."

Savanna glanced over at Joe's dour expression. He hardly looked as though he wanted to get on a first-name basis with her. After all, she was his secretary. Being here in his home tonight didn't change that fact.

Looking to Megan, she said, "Well, Megan, since your father is my boss, I—"

Suddenly Joe's voice interrupted. "If Ms. Starr doesn't mind I'll call her Savanna," he said to Megan, then arched an inquiring brow at Savanna. "And you may call me Joe. That is, if you want to," he added in a lazy, taunting way.

"That's, uh, fine," she told him, trying her best to sound casual, even though his suggestion was whirling all sorts of implications through her head.

He'd invited her to call him Joe, she thought with amazement. Only minutes after she'd met him, she'd thought of him as simply Joe. Yet to call him by that name seemed such an intimate thing to do. Which was silly, she told herself. He was just a man, not unlike any other man she'd worked for.

Who was she fooling? a little voice inside her groaned. Joe wasn't like any man she'd ever known in her entire life. Including Terry.

Drawing in a much-needed breath, Savanna finally managed to pull her eyes off him and look around the large dining room.

"Your home is beautiful, Joe. Have you lived here long?"

"Ever since I was a small child."

"Daddy and Mommy lived here when I was born," Megan put in. "That was a long time ago."

"Yes, you are getting to be an old lady," he told her, the hard line of his mouth suddenly softened by an indulgent little grin.

Savanna glanced at Joe and was immediately surprised by the deep affection she saw on his face. Not that she hadn't already decided that he loved his daughter. She just hadn't expected him to show it. Especially in front of his secretary.

"I'm thirteen," Megan reminded him.

Joe groaned, albeit good-naturedly. Savanna laughed and said, "I think we were living in Boston when I was thirteen. I'm not sure, since we'd probably lived in a dozen places by then. But I do remember my boyfriend at that time. He had orange-red hair and a freckled face, and he chewed bubble gum all the time."

"Ugh," Megan groaned with distaste. "He sounds gross. Why did you like him?"

Even though Megan had asked the question, she could feel Joe watching her, waiting for her answer as though she were about to reveal some deep dark secret about herself.

She shifted uncomfortably on the seat and told herself he wasn't really interested in her or her childhood. He was merely being polite.

"Because he was very nice to me," she answered Megan's question. "And we had lots of fun playing tennis together."

"Having fun is important to you, isn't it, Ms.—I mean, Savanna?" he asked.

Vexed by the tone of his voice, she looked at him. "You make it sound like having fun is committing a crime."

"Not at all. It's just more important to some than others."

"Life is too short not to gather as much enjoyment from it as possible," she said with conviction.

Joe couldn't remember the last time he'd really enjoyed living. His college days, perhaps? Before he'd married Deirdre? When he'd still believed he was going to have a meaningful career in geoscience and a family to call his own. That was a long time ago, he thought cynically, before he'd learned what life was really all about.

"I like playing tennis, too," Megan spoke up. "So does my mom. She taught me how."

Savanna would have been surprised if the young girl had said her father had taught her how to play the game. Even though he looked very athletic, she couldn't imagine Joe doing anything so frivolous as playing sports.

"You must be missing her," Savanna said.

Megan shrugged as though her mother being out of her life was no big deal, but the lost look on her face told Savanna otherwise.

"A little. But I got a letter from her today and that was nice."

"I'll bet she's missing you as much as you are her," Savanna said gently.

Megan shrugged again. "Well, she's really busy now unpacking everything. Did Daddy tell you that she moved to Africa? Near the Congo?"

Surprised to hear that the former Mrs. McCann had totally left the country, Savanna glanced at Joe, then back to his daughter. "No. He didn't. Does she plan on living over there for long?"

"At least for the next five years. You see, my stepdad is a doctor and he wants to volunteer his services. I wanted to go with them, but Mom said no way. She's going to be living where there's not any modern schools or anything like that for me to go to. Besides, she thought it was time for me to live with Daddy."

Savanna didn't know whether to feel sad for Megan because she'd had to tell her mother goodbye, or glad for Joe because he was finally getting the chance to be a father to his daughter. Either way, it couldn't be easy for the two of them to suddenly be thrust together after all these years of being apart.

Joe laid his fork across his empty salad plate. "Megan, you and Savanna look as though you're almost finished with your salad. Why don't you go get the main course from the kitchen."

"Sure. I'll be right back."

"Do you need my help?" Savanna asked as Megan jumped to her feet.

"No, thank you. I can manage. You just keep Daddy company."

She disappeared from the room and Savanna found herself alone with Joe. Yet being here with him like this was nothing like sitting in the office of McCann Drilling. This was his home and he'd invited her here. She was trying not to put too much stock in that, but she couldn't entirely forget it.

"That girl is so—"

Joe's voice broke off helplessly and Savanna laughed. "She is totally unlike you. I can tell you that."

He frowned. "Should I take that as a compliment to Megan or an insult to me?"

A smile still on her face, Savanna shook her head and reached for her water glass. "It was just an observation. Megan is a lovely girl. I like her. I like you, too. It's just that the two of you are very different."

His eyes dropped to his plate and for a brief moment Savanna saw a shadow pass across his face. "Perhaps Megan would have been more like me if Deirdre and I had stayed together. Maybe it's good that she's not."

"Why do you say that?"

As he lifted his eyes back to her, his mouth twisted with cynicism. "Come on, Savanna, you and I both know I'm not really a likable person. I don't pretend to be."

No, she had to admit he wasn't an easy person to warm up to. But for some reason she had. She hadn't lied when she'd told him she liked him. She did. Something about Joe McCann touched her. And that scared the very part of Savanna she'd carefully locked away from the world when Terry had died.

"How old was Megan when you divorced?" she asked him.

"Three. Since then I've had a weekend here and there with her and a couple of weeks in the summer."

The regret she heard in his voice tore at Savanna. "Well, obviously your ex-wife doesn't want to keep Megan away from you."

"No, Deirdre never tried to keep me from our daughter. Our divorce wasn't a bitter one. We both decided we simply had different goals in life. I—well, I just wish we could have made it work for Megan's sake."

Was he really wishing that for Megan or for himself, Savanna wondered. Maybe he was still in love with the woman. Was that why he had such a bitter, cynical outlook on life, because he'd lost the woman he loved and couldn't get her back? No, Savanna didn't think that was the case. Joe didn't appear to be a man in love with anyone or anything.

"Staying together simply for the sake of a child doesn't always turn out for the best," she told him. "Besides, you've got your chance with Megan now."

Sighing, Joe put down the fork and leaned back in his chair. Savanna's gaze followed his strong arms as he crossed them across his chest.

"Yeah. I've got another chance with her now. But I don't know anything about teenaged girls."

Her smile was full of encouragement. "Neither does any other man until they raise one of their own."

"Don't anyone starve to death yet! I'm coming," Megan announced as she pushed her way through a swinging wooden door at the back of the room.

Megan's return with the food prevented Joe from saying more. He was glad. He'd already said too much to Savanna. He didn't know what the hell it was about her, but she had a way of making words spill out of his mouth that he'd never intended to say. If he wasn't very careful, Joe thought, she was going to have him behaving like a blabbering fool.

Along with the catfish fillets, Megan served hushpuppies, crowder peas and baked potatoes. While the three of them ate, the young girl chatted animatedly of the life she'd left in Dallas.

"Our house there wasn't nearly as big and nice as this one," Megan went on, "but it was okay with me. Mom said she never did like this house, anyway. It was too ostentatious for her taste. Whatever that word means. But personally, I'm beginning to like it. I mean, Grandfather Joseph was an oilman. He might as well have lived high on the hog."

Joe cleared his throat loudly and leveled a stern look at his daughter. "It's true your grandfather made a lot of money, Megan, but he spent much more than he should have. That should be a lesson to you."

Megan turned a pitifully innocent look on her father. "Well, he didn't die broke! And at least he knew how to enjoy himself." She glanced at Savanna and smiled mischievously. "My grandfather had a reputation of being Oklahoma City's J. R. Ewing."

Joe, who'd just taken a drink of water, coughed in earnest. "Megan, I want you to quit this exaggerating in front of Savanna! Your grandfather was nothing like J. R. Ewing. Besides, you're way too young to have even seen that TV show."

Megan shook her head at him. "We watched the reruns all the time and Mom took me out to the real ranch they used for the Ewing spread. I told all the other tourists there that my daddy was an oilman, too."

Even though Megan had spoken with a great amount of pride, Savanna fully expected Joe to explode. When he didn't, she ventured a glance at the end of the table and was surprised to see him shaking his head with wry resignation.

"I give up, Megan. Go ahead and tell Savanna my bank balance and anything else about our family that you think might interest her."

Megan giggled as she bit into a crusty hushpuppy. "Oh, Daddy, you're so funny. I don't know how much money you have in the bank. And even if I did, I wouldn't tell Savanna, 'cause I don't think she cares about that sort of thing. She's too nice.''

He turned a dry, almost comical look on Savanna. "My daughter doesn't realize you have a nose problem."

Savanna laughed softly and wrinkled her nose at him. "I'm not *that* nosy, Joe."

"Maybe she'd rather hear about how Grandfather Joseph threatened to write you out of the will when you married Mom?'' Megan eagerly suggested, her brown curls bouncing as she scooted to the edge of her seat.

Savanna turned arched brows on her boss. "Is that true? Did he really threaten to disinherit you?''

Joe grimaced. "He certainly did. He didn't want me getting married."

"Why?'' Savanna asked. "Because he didn't like your ex-wife, or was there some other reason?''

"He thought Mother was a fluff head,'' Megan spoke up. "That's what she always told me. But Daddy was more of a rebel back then and he didn't care if Grandfather wrote him off all that loot.''

Joe muttered something under his breath, while Savanna had to cover her mouth to keep from laughing at Megan's colorful explanation.

"I wasn't a rebel,'' Joe informed his daughter. "A rebel is someone who constantly defies authority."

"Well, maybe you weren't a rebel,'' Megan conceded, "but there was that other time you told him what's what and went to work for that other oil company. Grandmother said it was the smartest thing you'd ever done.''

Bending his head, Joe closed his eyes and pinched the bridge of his nose. "Megan, if your grandmother McCann said that, then she didn't know what she was talking about. That particular oil company went broke and I eventually had to go back to McCann's. So you see, it's never wise to go against your father's advice," he said.

"But fathers can be wrong, Daddy. Grandmother McCann said Joseph wasn't the god you thought he was."

Apparently Joe thought his daughter had gone too far this time. Leveling a threatening glare at her, he said with a growl, "It's a good thing your grandmother doesn't live around here, otherwise she'd be feeding your head with more nonsense. Now be quiet and eat, young lady."

Megan obediently snapped her mouth shut, ducked her head, then spoiled the whole effect by looking across to Savanna and giving her a conspiratorial wink.

Chapter Six

After supper Joe excused himself to make a telephone call. With her father out of the way, Megan invited Savanna to her bedroom, where the teenager proudly showed her the collection of posters she had pinned to the wall, a stack of CDs and a closet full of clothes. Once that was finished, Megan decided Savanna needed a tour through the remainder of the house.

As Savanna walked through the large, richly furnished rooms, she was inclined to agree with the former Mrs. McCann. The place was a little too much for her taste. It was all very beautiful, but it certainly didn't have a warm, inviting feel to it. But then, maybe that was because Joe had lived alone for so long the house had forgotten how to be a home.

In order not to disturb Joe's phone call, the two of them avoided the small study he used as a home office and eventually wound up in the living room. With her arm still looped through Savanna's, the teenager guided her toward the fireplace where several photos graced the rock mantel.

Taking one down, she handed it to Savanna. "This was my grandfather Joseph," she said proudly. "He's almost as handsome as Daddy, don't you think? Mom says I have a personality just like him. But I don't know if that's true or not. I was only six when he died and I wasn't around him that much."

Savanna studied the man standing at the base of a massive oil rig. Like Joe, he was a tall, lean man. Because he was wearing a hard hat, it was impossible to see the color of his hair, but from the look of his tanned complexion she assumed it was similar to Joe's. His arm was slung casually around the shoulders of the man standing next to him. They were both giving the camera wide, toothy grins, as though they'd just hit pay dirt. She wondered if Joe had ever looked like this. Like a man happy and proud of his accomplishment.

"He was a very handsome man," Savanna quietly agreed.

Megan took the framed photo and handed her another. "This was Daddy a long time ago when I was just a baby," Megan explained.

Savanna studied the young Joe in the colored photo. He was a bit thinner, his tawny hair longer on his collar, but the most startling difference apparent to Savanna was his face. There were no obvious lines of stress and fatigue. Even a smile dimpled his lean cheeks.

"What was he doing with this strange-looking truck?" Savanna asked curiously.

"Oh, that's a seismograph buggy. You see, Daddy is actually a scientist. In that picture he'd been making tests to see if that section of land might have gas or oil beneath it."

Totally surprised, Savanna looked up at Megan. "Joe is a scientist?"

Megan nodded. "He knows all about seismology and he has a degree in geochemistry. I don't know exactly what all that is, but I do know that it used to be really important to him. Now he doesn't do it anymore because Grandfather Joseph died and he had to take over the business part of the drilling company."

Savanna glanced down at the photo in her hands. Joe certainly looked as if he was in his element here, she thought. "Your father didn't mention he was a scientist. But then, I've only been his secretary for a few days."

Megan's young voice was suddenly tinged with sadness. "I'm not surprised. Daddy doesn't talk about it anymore. He says that part of his life is over."

Savanna continued to study Joe's seemingly happy face in the photo. "Hmm. I can't imagine wasting all that education," she murmured thoughtfully.

"That's what Grandmother McCann says. She thinks Daddy would be much happier if he was doing geology work like he used to."

Savanna handed the photo back to Megan. "And what do you think?"

Megan shrugged, then turned and positioned the photo back on the mantel. "Oh, he doesn't talk to me about work much. But then, Daddy's not a talker. Unless he's laying down rules I'm supposed to follow, then he goes overboard with the talk. But I know he doesn't like his job."

"What makes you say that?"

Megan grimaced. "Because every night he comes home like a bear. He either needs a different job or another wife. But I haven't figured out how to convince him of that yet."

Another wife? Savanna couldn't picture Joe with a woman. At least, not in the family-type way Megan was thinking of. Or was it that she simply didn't want to think of Joe with a woman?

Shaking the disturbing question out of her mind, Savanna asked, "Would you like to have a stepmother?"

A wide smile spread across the young girl's face. "Yeah! I'd like to have a brother or sister and since Mom isn't going to have any more babies it's all up to Daddy."

Savanna breathed in deeply and told herself it meant nothing to her if Joe married and had another child. It was none of her business. But the whole idea bothered her. Much more than she ever cared to admit. "Uh, have you told Joe that you'd like to have a brother or sister?"

Giggling impishly, Megan shook her head. "Only that he should get married again. Not the brother or sister part. But when I find the right woman for him I will."

Before Savanna could even think of a reply to that, Megan latched onto her arm once again and tugged her away from the fireplace. "Let's go to the kitchen. If you'd like you can make coffee. Daddy probably won't be off the phone for ages yet."

Megan's prediction turned out to be true. It was nearly an hour later when Joe appeared in the kitchen. By then Savanna was thinking it was time for her to go home. She'd already had a long, enlightening visit with Megan. As for Joe, she hadn't been invited here tonight to spend time with him.

"Sorry I was on the phone so long," he said to Savanna as he took a seat beside her at a small breakfast bar. "But it was business."

Surprised that he was being apologetic, she said, "Think nothing of it. Megan has been showing me the house and how she decorated her room."

"With all those clothes, you mean?"

"Oh, Daddy," Megan groaned. "My bedroom isn't that bad. I'll bet Savanna's room was just as messy when she was my age."

The girl looked to Savanna for support, and Savanna had to laugh. "My bedroom is still messy," she confessed.

Joe wasn't surprised by this news. At work, Savanna's desk was already a mass of clutter, so it was easy to imagine what her bedroom looked like. The bedcovers would be tumbled, her dresser would be littered with bottles of perfume and makeup, satiny scraps of lingerie would be lying wherever she'd decided to take them off. Oh, yes, he thought, an uncomfortable heat rising up in him, he could picture Savanna's bedroom without any effort at all. Even worse, he could see Savanna in it, her feet bare, her hair mussed, her luscious curves barely covered with black lace.

"Daddy? Did you hear me?"

Megan's voice finally penetrated his thoughts, but he had no idea what she'd been saying to him. "Sorry, honey, I was thinking about... something else."

"I was talking about my room. Savanna said it looked okay to her. She says I should get marks for having the bed made, and for not having dirty dishes or food smashed into the carpet."

What in hell was going on? Joe suddenly wondered. One day Savanna Starr walks into his office, the next she's sitting in his home, influencing his daughter with her lax ideas about living and filling his head with crazy, erotic notions that could only lead him down a path of mental destruction. He had to stop this before it got out of hand.

"If you want good marks from me," he said to Megan, "you're going to have to get all those clothes up and get them packed into a suitcase. We've got to fly to Houston on Monday."

Surprised, Savanna looked over at him. Even though Joe had mentioned that he sometimes had to travel out of town, she hadn't expected it to be so soon.

"You're leaving this Monday?" She blurted the question.

Joe nodded. "That's what the call was about. I've got to meet with a few businessmen. Leonard Brown in particular. He's thinking about contracting McCann's to drill a well in eastern Oklahoma."

"Oh. Well, that's good," she said, wondering why she suddenly felt so deflated. "I mean, that is what you want, isn't it? More work."

Feeling as though the space between their bar stools had shrunk to an inch or two, Joe got to his feet, moved over to the cabinets and leaned against the counter. "Yeah. That's exactly what I need."

He didn't sound very enthusiastic. But what did Savanna know about it? The man didn't seem to get excited about anything, except his secretary being late for work.

"Why do I have to go?" Megan groaned the question at him. "I don't want to stay in some stuffy motel room while you talk to a bunch of old men. It'll be boring, boring."

Sighing, he said, "There's no point in arguing, Megan. You're far too young to be left at home alone. You're coming with me."

Megan, who was perched on a step-chair, jumped to her feet and folded her arms against her chest. "I won't go!" she said defiantly. "Not unless Savanna comes with us!"

Savanna jerked her head around to see Joe staring at his daughter in disbelief.

"Megan, don't be difficult. Savanna needs to be here to keep the office open."

Megan's chin jutted stubbornly outward. "Then I'm staying here, too!"

Muttering a curse under his breath, Joe walked over to his daughter and laid a hand on her shoulder. "Don't be childish about this, Megan. There's no reason to drag Savanna to Houston with us.''

The teenager whirled away from him, then flounced over to the bar and plopped down beside Savanna. "If Savanna went with us, I'd have someone to talk to. It wouldn't be boring and lonely.''

Joe tilted his head back and stared helplessly at the ceiling. Did all teenagers think it was their God-given right to be entertained every minute of the day? he wondered.

"You could try talking to me," he suggested.

Megan's head whipped back and forth. "You'll either be studying a bunch of reports or talking to those oilmen.''

Joe could hardly argue that point. The majority of the time spent in Houston he would be reading reports or talking to businessmen. Still, Megan needed to know she couldn't always have her way.

Deciding it was time to change tactics, Megan said, "Daddy, Savanna really should go for your sake, anyway.''

Joe's expression turned mocking. "She needs to go for my sake?''

"That's right," she said smugly, then smiled at Savanna, who appeared to be totally bewildered by it all. "If you have your personal secretary at the meeting with you to take notes and all that stuff, it'll make you look more... well, more important.''

Joe studied Megan through narrowed eyes. She was stubborn and contrary, yet she was also smart in ways that reminded him of Joseph. To have Savanna with him would make a better impression. A man who could afford his secretary to travel with him didn't run a fly-by-night drilling business, and Leonard Brown was a man who took note of everything. Maybe this was the right time to listen to his daughter, he pondered.

Turning his gaze on Savanna, he allowed himself a lingering look at her sultry brown eyes, the sensual curve of her lips, then finally her shapely legs. He'd be lying if he said he didn't enjoy the sight of her. He also had to admit there was a foolish part of him that wanted Savanna's company on this trip, too.

"You're right, honey," he said to Megan, though he continued to look at Savanna. "I think Savanna should go with us."

Savanna's mouth virtually dropped open. "Joe, I think—"

Before she could say more, Megan squealed loudly and threw her arms around Savanna's neck.

"Isn't it great, Savanna? You're going to Houston with us!" Jumping to her feet she ran over to Joe, hugged his waist, then hopped on her toes and kissed his cheek. "Thanks, Daddy!" she cried excitedly. "You're wonderful!"

A joyous smile lighted her face and Joe was amazed at how good it felt to make his daughter happy. Maybe he was spoiling her, but for now he wasn't going to worry about it. He actually felt a little happy himself.

"I'm wonderful?" he asked wryly. "I thought you said I was a stuffed shirt?"

Megan giggled. "Well, not always," she said, then, turning, she raced toward the hallway and her bedroom. "I'm going to start packing right now!"

Once the girl was gone from the room, it was absurdly quiet, as though a tornado had just ripped things apart and the dust was silently drifting down to the rubble.

"Joe, I think—"

"Savanna, I know—"

They both spoke at the same time.

Laughing, Savanna spread her palms upward in a gesture of invitation. "You go first," she told him.

Now that the two of them were alone, reality was settling in on Joe. None of what he'd just done made sense. Sure, he'd let Megan's reasoning validate taking Savanna to Houston with him. But who was he kidding? He was becoming addicted to the sight, the sound, the simple presence of Savanna Starr. And that disturbed the hell out of him.

Raking a hand through his hair, he said, "I was just going to say that I know you probably hadn't expected to be traveling out of town on this job. But I would consider it a favor if you would agree to go. Of course, I'll pay all your expenses and overtime wages for the extra work."

He made it sound so businesslike, Savanna thought. So why didn't she think of the whole thing as simply a job she was being asked to do?

"I don't want overtime. That isn't necessary. But I do wonder what made you change your mind. Earlier, I got the impression you didn't want me to go," she couldn't help saying.

Joe moved away from the row of cabinets and Savanna's eyes followed him as he walked around the large room. He hadn't dressed for dinner tonight. He was wearing faded jeans, a plain white T-shirt and the same boots he wore to work. As she watched the muscles of his back flex beneath the thin cotton, she decided Marlon Brando should never have worn that T-shirt all those years ago in *On the Waterfront*. Now men like Joe went around in them, turning a girl's thinking to a pile of mush. It was decadent.

"Well, I saw how much it meant to Megan," he said, "and I realized it would be better for you to go and keep her pacified than to have you stay here and run the office."

"Is that the only reason?"

He stopped his pacing and looked at her. Savanna felt a jolt as his blue eyes connected with hers.

"That, and you will be a help to me at the meeting. There's always a lot of numbers to present at one of these things." His brows pulled together in a quizzical frown as he noted a flicker of doubt on her face. "Why? What other reason would I have for asking you to go?"

Savanna had never been a nervous person, but something was making her decidedly edgy. She wasn't sure if it was the way Joe's blue eyes kept sliding over her or simply the fact that she was going out of town with him.

Sliding off the bar stool, she smoothed a hand down the front of her dress. "Uh—forget I asked. Right now I'd better get home. When did you plan on leaving?"

"I've already called Will Rogers Airport. There's a flight leaving for Houston at eight thirty-five Monday morning. We'll need to be there in plenty of time to get our tickets and check in."

Even though there were all sorts of doubts about this trip whirling around in Savanna's head, she nodded and gave him the cheeriest smile she could muster. "I'll be ready."

Walking over to her, he said, "I'm going to have a cup of coffee. Would you like to join me before you leave?"

A giant yes was in her throat just screaming to get out, but Savanna determinedly tamped it down and shook her head. She was already spending too much time with the man and thinking things about him that were definitely dangerous. No, she needed to go home, regroup and convince herself that she could make this trip with him and Megan and still keep her senses intact.

"Thank you, but I drank a cup earlier."

He shrugged. "Then I'll walk you to your car."

Suddenly wary of his unexpected show of manners tonight, Savanna glanced up at him. "Oh, that isn't necessary. I can find my way back out."

Joe reached out and took hold of her upper arm. "I'll
walk with you anyway," he said, his expression quietly daring her to protest.

Too stunned to argue, Savanna allowed him to lead her
out of the house and down the driveway to her car.

Once they were standing beside the little orange car, Savanna turned to face him. "Please tell Megan how much I
enjoyed meeting her."

He studied her for a long moment. "I think you really did
enjoy my daughter tonight."

She frowned at him. "You sound surprised."

Joe knew there wasn't any logical reason to keep holding
her arm. But he did anyway. Her skin was like warm satin
against his fingers and he knew if he were to lean down and
touch his lips to hers, he would find them even softer.

"I didn't know how you'd take her. She's— I'll put it this
way, discretion never enters her head before she opens her
mouth."

An indulgent smile curved her lips. "Well, it's obvious
she's very proud of you."

Joe grimaced. "I don't know why. In the fathering department I've let her down more often than not."

He was selling himself short as a father, Savanna mused
sadly, just as he seemed to sell himself short as a drilling
contractor. What could possibly have gone so wrong in his
life to make him think in such a way?

"I don't know about that," Savanna said. "But I do
know that simply spending time with her is really what Megan wants from you."

The tips of his fingers began to move ever so slightly
against the side of her arm. Savanna didn't know if he was

aware of what he was doing, but to her it was an intimate, inviting touch and one she knew she should pull away from. But to be this close to him with the night cloaking them with damp heat was mesmerizing, making it impossible for her to move.

"And how do you know that?" he asked. "Is that what she told you?"

"No. But I'm a daughter. I know. Our daddy is the first man we fall in love with. Megan needs to know you love her back."

Joe grimaced. "Megan thinks loving her is letting her go to public school."

Savanna's brows lifted, then soft laughter parted her lips. "Maybe it is, Joe."

It wouldn't do for him to spend very much time around this woman, he realized. She had an easy way about her that made him want to relax, let his guard down and say to hell with the worries on his shoulders.

"Not in my opinion. I want her to have more than what a public school can offer."

"Megan might want something else," Savanna observed.

Joe made an impatient sound in his throat. "Of course she does. She wants to go to proms and dances."

Savanna's brows lifted in disbelief, then, laughing, she grabbed hold of both his hands. "There's nothing wrong with dancing, Joe. In fact, there's much to be said for dancing."

"Yeah, and it's all negative," he said, his face marred with a frown.

Savanna laughed again. "You do know how to dance, don't you, Joe?"

She was holding on to his hands, clasping them to hers as though she'd known him for years. Joe knew he should pull away from her and put an end to this nonsense. But her touch was seductive, and her laughter soothed the frayed edges of his heart.

"A little," he muttered reluctantly.

Tightening her hands around his, she cast a daring look up at him. "Show me."

"Wh-what?" he stuttered with disbelief.

"Show me you can dance. Whirl me around the driveway and I'll explain all the good points of dancing."

"You're crazy."

She smiled at him. "I know. But I'm not dangerous. I promise."

She was dangerous. Especially to his peace of mind. But tonight, just for the moment he wasn't going to think about that.

Drawing her into his arms, he guided her into a simple two-step. "If the neighbors look out and see us, they'll probably call the cops."

Savanna giggled. "No, they'll just be angry because they weren't invited to the party."

"We're having a party?" he asked mockingly as they moved around the concrete driveway.

"It feels like it to me."

Joe couldn't tell her what it felt like to him. To have his hand spanning the side of her waist, the tips of her breasts brushing against his chest, was filling him with an urge to simply crush his mouth onto hers until he was drunk on the taste of her.

"So what are these benefits of dancing you were going to enlighten me on?"

Like the fingers of a lover, shadows were touching his cheeks and lips. Savanna had to fight the urge to cover those shadows with her own fingers, to draw his head down to hers and kiss his mouth until it softened and smiled back at her.

"Well, of course, the most obvious is the physical exercise, then there's hand and foot coordination," she said as she desperately tried to shake herself back to reality.

"Jumping rope will achieve the same results," he observed.

Savanna shook her head hopelessly. "Maybe so, but dancing teaches other things like... personal relations."

His brows lifted skeptically and Savanna's lips spread into a provocative smile. "Well, we are relating, aren't we? One on one?"

If she thought he'd allow Megan to learn this sort of personal relating, she was out of her mind. And what the hell was he doing, anyway, dancing his secretary around on the driveway without one note of music?

He stopped abruptly and dropped his hands away from her. Savanna looked up at him questioningly.

"Well, isn't that enough proof for you?"

"Proof?" she asked, her hands still resting against the middle of his chest.

Irritated at the blank, dreamy look on her face, he snapped, "Proof that I can dance, damn it!"

His sudden change of voice snapped Savanna back to the present and she jumped back from him as if he were a hot coal. "Oh, well, yes, I believe you must have danced once or twice. Years ago, when you were young."

Incredulous, Joe stared at her as he tried to figure out what had insulted him the most. The idea that she thought he was old, or that he couldn't dance. "Ms.—I mean, Savanna, you—"

She shook her head. "I didn't mean for that to sound critical. But I would have enjoyed a few twirls and dips."

Joe would like to dip her, he thought, right over the hood of that orange car of hers. Before he let her up, she'd know she'd been kissed. And she'd definitely know he wasn't old!

"But we can do that next time," he heard her saying.

Next time? Joe would run like hell before he allowed her to talk him into anything like this again.

"I doubt it. I'm not too big on dips and twirls."

Laughing, Savanna climbed into her car and shut the door. Yet when she looked out the window at him, the smile on her face was touched with regret. "That's not surprising."

"What's that supposed to mean?" he asked, annoyed with himself because he didn't yet want her to go. She exasperated him, but she also made him feel good. And that didn't make a lick of sense.

"It means that if we were a comedy team, you'd always have to be the straight man, Joe. And when I say straight, I mean starched-stiff straight."

"Well, fortunately for you, we have to run a drilling company together, not play a Vegas nightclub."

Laughing, Savanna clapped her hands together. "You made a joke, Joe! A dry one, I admit. But I liked it."

Before Joe could say anything to that, she started the engine then reversed the car onto the street. With a little wave she called, "See you in the morning."

Joe lifted his hand in acknowledgment, then turned and started back to the house. It wasn't until he reached the porch that he burst out laughing.

Immediately the light over his head flashed on and Megan opened the front door in his face.

"Daddy, is something wrong out here?"

Joe smiled at his daughter. "No. Everything is fine. Why?"

"I thought I heard a noise. Like someone laughing."

Dear Lord, he thought, laughter was such a rare thing around this house, his own daughter thought something was wrong when she heard it.

"That was me. I just told Savanna a joke before she left."

Surprise widened Megan's blue eyes. "You told a joke? Daddy, are you feeling all right?"

Stepping into the house, Joe curled his arm around his daughter's shoulders. "I feel fine, honey."

In fact, for the first time in a long time Joe felt relaxed, almost happy. Had one evening with Savanna Starr done that to him? Dear God, he hoped not. Otherwise, this trip to Houston was going to get him into deep trouble.

Chapter Seven

Savanna crossed her legs and glanced out the window of the DC-9. Finally, after a forty-minute delay, the rain and lightning had finally quieted to a harmless drizzle. In a matter of minutes the plane would be airborne and on its way to Houston.

"Are you afraid to fly, Savanna?"

Savanna turned her head toward the deep sound of Joe's voice and was suddenly taken by the fact that he seemed so close to her. She'd never noticed the seats on this particular airline being so jammed together before. Joe's knee was only inches from hers and his face so near she could see the little flecks of dark blue circling the pupil of his eyes, the faint shadow of rust red whiskers beneath his skin.

"No. I like to fly," she answered.

Joe's eyes dropped to her hands. "I wasn't sure. The way you were tugging and twisting your fingers together, I thought you might be a little anxious about taking off."

She *was* anxious about taking off with him! After she'd driven home to her apartment Friday night, she'd lain awake for hours, remembering how it had felt to be touched by him, the way his face had looked down at her as he'd danced her around the driveway. And she hadn't forgotten anything over the weekend. He was getting to her. She didn't know why or how he was doing it. She only knew that when she looked at him now, she saw an altogether different man than the one who had growled at her for being late. Last week she'd wanted to bop him over the head for that. Now she wanted to kiss him. It was crazy!

Smiling, Savanna did her best to sound as breezy as she could. "Oh, no. I'm fine. Just wondering what Houston will be like. I've been there before. But that was years ago."

"I can tell you what Houston will be like in three words," he said blandly.

Her eyebrows peaked as she studied his face. "Really. Tell me."

"Huge, hot and humid."

Disappointed, Savanna grimaced. "Is that all?"

"That's all I've ever noticed."

"I'm not surprised," she murmured.

His silent look demanded she explain. Savanna licked her lips and said, "I mean, you don't seem very interested in the superficial look of things."

Hell, Joe silently cursed, what did she know? He was sitting here now wondering how he was going to keep his eyes off her long enough to persuade Leonard Brown and his business cronies it was time to drill for gas.

She was a beautiful woman. But then, he'd come to that conclusion the moment she'd first walked into his office with grease marks on her dress and face. Today she was wearing pink silk. At least, Joe believed it was silk. Whatever the fabric, it was soft and flimsy and so thin that when she moved a certain way he could see the texture of her lace bra beneath it.

As if that weren't enough to distract him, her skirt certainly finished the job. It was close fitting, cream colored and came to a stop just below her knees. The left side of it, the one next to Joe, was split upon her leg. And even though the opening was supplied with buttons and buttonholes, she'd obviously decided to leave them all undone.

Joe was finding it hard indeed to keep from reaching over and fastening the whole thing back together. At least then he might be able to look at something besides her thigh.

A few minutes later the plane began to taxi down the runway, then pick up speed. Joe glanced across the aisle at Megan to make sure she had her seat belt safely fastened, then back at Savanna, who was waving out the window. "I don't think anyone can see you from here, Savanna," he said dryly.

The plane lifted smoothly into the air and the Will Rogers Airport was suddenly behind them. Savanna turned away from the window to look at Joe. "Well, my friend Jenny is down there and I promised I'd wave goodbye."

"You're only going to be gone for one night," he observed.

She gave him a wan smile. "Yes, I know, but Jenny thinks you might be devious and lecherous and that you're really more interested in my body than you are in signing a contract."

Joe stared at her blankly, as though her words had been just too much for his mind to absorb.

Savanna gave her hand an inconsequential wave, then recrossed her legs. "Frankly, I told her that was the most hilarious thing I'd ever heard. Don't you think so, too?"

He grimaced. "Can't you see me dying of laughter?"

Even though he looked like a judge about to hand down a life sentence without parole, Savanna began to chuckle. "Don't worry, Joe, I told her I didn't think you liked women. At least, not in that way."

Glancing over at Megan, Joe was relieved to see his daughter had on earphones and couldn't hear their conversation. "In other words, you cut my masculinity to shreds."

Her lips parted with surprise. "Not really. I mean, she knows you have a daughter and that you obviously...liked women thirteen years ago."

"It was so nice of you to explain all of that to her. I really like the idea that you discussed my sex habits with someone I don't even know," he voiced sarcastically.

Savanna shot him an offended look. "I wasn't discussing you. I was defending you. Or did you want her to think you really are lecherous? Besides," she went on before he could answer, "I don't know anything about your sex habits."

"That's right, you don't. And that's the way it's going to stay," he assured her.

"I wouldn't even pretend to be interested," she said, then turned away from him and reached for a magazine on the back of the seat. Quickly she flipped through the pages without seeing them, then, heaving out a short breath, she looked back over at Joe. "Maybe I shouldn't say anything but—well, now that we've managed to get on the subject of sex, I think you ought to know that Megan is hoping you'll give her a brother or sister."

Joe twisted around in his seat so that his stunned face was only inches from Savanna's. "Did I hear you right?"

Savanna's eyes roamed over the lean, bony angles of his features, the provocative line of his lips, then finally settled on his piercing blue gaze. Oh, yes, she thought, there were plenty of women who would find him attractive, and even more who would be willing to marry him and give him a child. Did he realize that? she wondered.

Nodding, Savanna said, "She wants a sibling, and since her mother has no intentions of giving her one, she's pinned her hopes on you."

Joe's head swung back and forth in disbelief. "That's ridiculous. And she shouldn't have been discussing it with you, anyway."

Savanna told herself not to be insulted. After all, he was probably in a small state of shock and didn't realize what he was saying. "Who should she be discussing it with?"

"Me," he retorted, tapping his fist against his chest.

Savanna gave him a patient smile. "She intends to. But right now she's probably afraid you'd just tell her to forget it."

"Damn right I would. I'm not interested in getting married again. Ever. One mistake was enough for me."

Savanna could understand that. After Terry had died she'd sworn herself off the idea of marriage. She wasn't about to put her faith and hope into another man and suddenly have it all stripped away for a third time. And so far she hadn't met a man who'd been able to make her think any differently.

However, these past couple of months since she'd started a life of her own, there had been more and more times Savanna had imagined what it might be like if she had a husband who loved her, and a baby of her own. But that kind of thinking was hazardous to her heart and she tried not to dwell on it. She'd had her chances with love and lost. Now she had to focus all her attention on finishing her education and becoming a CPA.

Joe leaned back in his seat and pinched the bridge of his nose. "Why would Megan want a brother or sister, anyway?" he muttered after a few moments. "Her mother and

I have tried to give her most everything she's ever asked for."

Savanna's gaze slanted across to her boss. "Apparently not the things she really wanted. She obviously wants for you and her to be a real family."

Joe's expression was almost pained as he glanced over at Savanna. "We are a real family," he reasoned.

The man just didn't get it, she thought sadly. He viewed everything logically, not emotionally. It was no wonder he couldn't bend, couldn't laugh, couldn't love.

"If you say so, Joe."

Several hours later Joe shook hands with Leonard Brown and his associates as they filed out of the small conference room. Nearby, Savanna gathered the notes and reports her boss had used at the meeting.

"Well," she said when he was finally able to join her back at the long table. "This has turned into a profitable day for you."

Joe picked up the stack of papers she'd neatly arranged and stuffed them into his briefcase. "It looks that way," he said flatly.

Annoyed by his lack of enthusiasm, she exclaimed, "Looks that way! My word, Joe, you just agreed to a contract to drill not just one well, but two! I think it's wonderful."

Joe snapped the briefcase shut. "Are you ready to go? I've got to get back to my room and make a bunch of phone calls."

Stung by his shortness, Savanna merely nodded and followed him out of the room. Once in the corridor, he punched the elevator button, then glanced over his shoulder at her.

"What are you going to do now?"

Savanna didn't know why he bothered asking. He obviously wasn't interested in her comings and goings. In fact, ever since she'd told him about Megan wanting a sibling, he'd seemed to distance himself from her.

Well, if hearing the truth bothered him that much, Savanna couldn't help it. She wasn't going to stop speaking her mind just because he didn't like what she had to say. The man needed to wake up and see the world around him!

"Megan has been up in her room ever since we got here. I'm going to go do something with her."

"Like what?"

Savanna bristled at his skeptical tone. Apparently he believed she didn't have any sense of proper behavior for herself or a young teenaged girl. And why? Simply because she could laugh at life? Because she didn't live by his rigid standards?

"Oh, I don't know, Joe, maybe we'll put on Lycra dresses, black fishnet hose and high heels, then hit the streets of Houston and see what we can find."

His face turned dark red. "I don't find that amusing."

Her brows lifted mockingly. "That's not surprising. You don't find anything amusing. Now, if you'll excuse me, I think I'll take the stairs."

She was halfway up the first flight when Joe appeared beside her. Not bothering to glance over at him, Savanna continued to climb.

"I don't want you and Megan leaving the hotel," he said.

"Why not just go ahead and narrow it down to our room?" she asked flippantly.

He made a sound of frustration. "This crabbiness isn't like you, Savanna. Or maybe it is. Maybe I just don't know you."

"No, you don't know me," she said, her voice becoming a bit winded. "Otherwise, you would instinctively know that you could trust me to take good care of your daughter. And not lead her down a path of corruption!''

"I didn't think that. I don't think it! I just don't want you two out of the hotel. At least, not without me. It isn't safe and I don't want anything happening to either of you."

"Fine," she returned. "Whatever we do, we won't go far."

Joe didn't say anything else until they reached the landing of the eighth floor, then he turned and put his hand on Savanna's shoulder.

She looked at him questioningly and was surprised to see his expression had softened.

"I just wanted to thank you for your help in the meeting. Leonard was impressed with you."

It was the first sign of appreciation he'd given her since she'd gone to work for him, and Savanna felt her earlier frustration with him drain away as quickly as it had come.

"It's just my job, Joe," she said, then, smiling, she reached out and patted his chest. "As for you, I think you'd better get out from behind your desk and do something physical. You're breathing a little hard, Mr. McCann."

Joe groaned as he watched the swing of her hips as she walked away. He was breathing hard, all right. But she was the cause of it. Not seven flights of stairs!

Megan was delighted with Savanna's idea of going down to the hotel gym. After a workout with weights, the treadmill, the stair climber and the rowing machine, they donned bathing suits and soaked in the hot tub.

When their skin finally began to shrivel and Savanna had regained her strength, the two of them dressed and went down to the lobby in search of a beauty salon.

As they sat waiting on plush pink chairs and looking through glamour magazines, Megan reached over and squeezed Savanna's hand.

"This is really fun, Savanna. Thanks for coming on this trip. Now that Mommy's gone, I don't get to do stuff like this."

Savanna's heart melted at the happy sparkle in Megan's eyes. Perhaps the girl had been blessed with financial security and the things it could buy. But she needed more than that. She needed love and a sense of belonging.

"I'm glad you're enjoying it, Megan."

"I've never had a manicure in a salon before," she said with a giggle. "Do you think Daddy will mind?"

Savanna gave the teenager a reassuring smile. "If he does, I'll bring him down here and make him get one."

Megan laughed. "That's really funny, Savanna." Then, her expression suddenly serious, she asked, "Do you like my daddy?"

Savanna shrugged. "Yes. Most of the time. Other times I don't like him at all."

"Yeah, I know what you mean. I don't like him when he's giving me long-winded lectures," Megan said glumly. "When do you not like him?"

"When he's being bossy," Savanna answered without hesitation.

"But, Savanna," she said, her face a comical puzzle, "Daddy is your boss."

Savanna looked over at the teenager. Megan was right, she thought. Joe was her boss and she'd best not let herself forget it.

Hours later Savanna sat on the restaurant balcony, staring out at the lighted skyline of Houston. She knew it was getting late and she should be heading back to her room. But she still felt restless and knew it would be futile to try to sleep.

Earlier in the evening she'd tried watching TV, but Savanna had never really been a television person and the only programs she could find were cop shows or sitcoms with bad acting. She liked baseball and eventually ran through the channels until she found a game already in the seventh inning. But the score was so lopsided she couldn't get interested. Finally she'd come up here to the restaurant and ordered a pot of coffee.

If she was going to be awake, she might as well be good and awake, she thought as she lifted her cup to her lips.

"What are you doing up here?"

The unexpected sound of Joe's voice startled her and coffee went splashing across the white linen tablecloth. "Damn!" she muttered, sopping the hot liquid from the back of her hand.

Joe quickly pulled out the wrought-iron chair next to hers and reached for her hand. "Did you burn yourself?"

"No. It's fine. Really," she assured him.

She quickly pulled her fingers from his and refilled her coffee cup from the insulated pot the waiter had left on the table. "Would you like a cup of this?"

He pushed the empty cup in front of him over to Savanna. "I thought you and Megan had retired for the night."

"You thought half right. Megan is fast asleep. I...just wasn't ready for bed yet." She glanced at him. "What are you doing up here?"

Shrugging, he glanced out at the darkened skyline. "It's been a long day. I thought I'd have a drink and unwind a bit before I went to bed."

"Then perhaps you'd better order something other than coffee," she suggested.

He took a careful sip of the hot liquid. "I doubt it will keep me from sleeping," he said. But she certainly would, he thought as his eyes glided over her features, which were softened even more by the flickering shadows around them. She was still wearing the dress she'd worn to supper to-night. It was light blue, thin and gauzy, and had a big white collar. If the neckline hadn't veed to the cleft between her breasts and the waist cinched in tightly to silhouette her curves, it would have been a sweet, demure dress, appro-priate for even the front pew at church. As it was, she looked flirty and sexy and too damned tempting for Joe's peace of mind.

"You, uh, were quiet at supper," Savanna remarked af-ter a few moments. "Is something wrong? Leonard didn't back out on the deal, did he?"

Joe stared into his coffee cup. "No. Everything is still on. In fact, I've already got the wheels in motion."

"That's good."

"Yeah."

The one flatly spoken word drew Savanna's eyes to his face and her heart sank as she realized nothing was there. No joy. No anger. It was as if he was anesthetized and had lost the ability to feel passionate about anything.

"I don't understand you, Joe. Today, after the meeting, you seemed—" Not really knowing what to say, she broke off with a shrug. "Well, it was like you didn't care if the deal had even taken place. And you don't seem any happier about it now."

He frowned at her. "Why do you keep harping about happy? My job has nothing to do with being happy."

Savanna's soft laughter was full of disbelief. "Do you al-ways go around lying to yourself?"

Sarcasm twisted his features. "Do you always go around trying to psychoanalyze people?"

She gave him a saucy grin as if to remind him his glowers and rough voice didn't daunt her. "Only when I think they need it."

"Well, I don't need it. I made a deal today to drill two new gas wells. What do you want me to do? Laugh and shout hallelujah?"

"It might be nice if you would. At least then I'd know you weren't a total iceberg."

If he were an iceberg, he would've already turned into a puddle of water, Joe thought miserably. Just looking at her overheated him. "Savanna, I've tried to get it over to you that I'm not the laughing, shouting hallelujah type. Never was. Never will be."

"Why not?"

With a heavy sigh he rose from the chair and walked over to the wrought-iron balustrade guarding the balcony. "I don't have time for such nonsense. Besides, why should I act thrilled over something that's barely going to make a dent in McCann's financial problems? God, I'd be ashamed to be happy," he muttered. "Especially when I know my father would have a fit if he could see the condition of the company today."

I'd be ashamed to be happy. Savanna had never heard anything so sad.

Rising from her chair, she went over to him. "You're wrong to keep putting yourself down, to keep blaming yourself for McCann's problems."

"Who should I blame, Savanna?" he asked bitterly.

His hand was clenched over the black iron railing. Savanna gently covered it with her own.

"You need to remember that you're flesh and blood, Joe. And no one expects you to be perfect. You need to wake up and realize that your father wasn't superhuman, or even J. R. Ewing. He just happened to be lucky enough to build a business when oil and gas prices were booming. If he were alive today, he'd be having the same troubles you are."

"I seriously doubt that," he muttered. "Joseph Mc-Cann was a shaker and a doer."

Savanna's hand tightened over his as every part of her longed to ease the anguish she knew he carried with him from day to day.

"You are a doer, too, Joe. You're just doing the wrong thing."

He pulled his eyes away from the lights in the distance to look at her. She was smiling at him, but that was no surprise. He'd come to expect her smile, to even look forward to its warmth and joy.

"You say that with such conviction," he said with a heavy sigh. "And I don't know why. You haven't known me long enough to make that sort of conjecture."

"How long does it take to know a person, Joe? A day? Several weeks or months?" Shaking her head, she turned and rested her back against the balustrade and looked up at the ink black sky. "My mother and father lived together for nearly twenty years and I don't think they ever really knew each other."

He glanced at her upturned face. "They weren't happy?"

"Well, on the surface, I guess you could say they were happy. At least they never wanted to divorce each other. But my mother was—" She sighed wistfully. "I don't know— she was never quite satisfied. You see, she always wanted more children, but she would never allow herself to get pregnant again. She'd say, not with the family moving from town to town. It would be too hard to raise a baby like that. So she kept putting off her dream, waiting for perfect conditions, until finally she was too old and health problems ruled out any hopes of her having more children."

Savanna looked at him, her expression resolute. "I learned something from her, Joe. You can't sit around, waiting for what you really want to come to you. A person has to work for it. Life will never be perfect or easy. My mother should have realized that, forged ahead and had a whole houseful of kids. Instead, she died never getting what she really wanted. I don't intend for that to happen to me. And I don't want it to happen to you."

With a muttered oath he turned away from her and stared down at the street several stories below them. "You think you've got it all figured out, don't you?"

"No," she said, determined not to let his bitterness put her off. She wanted to help him. She wanted him to believe in himself as a father and a man. "No. What I don't have figured out is why you feel so obligated to keep doing a job you don't even like."

How could she know so much about him? Was he that transparent, or was she able to see things about him that no one else could see?

"You don't understand, Savanna," he said gruffly. "McCann Drilling was my father's life blood and it was his wish for me to keep it going after he was gone. In fact, it was one of the last things he spoke about before he died. I gave him my promise and I can't go back on that now."

Moving closer, she gently touched his forearm. "I was told you should never make promises to a dying person. The promise might turn out to be too difficult to keep."

He looked at her, a wry expression twisting his features. "But when you love that dying person—well, I wanted to make him happy. I guess I still do."

"I can understand that."

"You couldn't. Not until you've been through it."

Drawing her hand away from his arm, Savanna closed her eyes. As Joe looked at her, he realized for the first time since he'd met her, he was seeing real pain on her face.

"I have been through it, Joe," she said quietly. "I lost someone I loved once. He wanted a promise from me, too. But I couldn't give it to him. Not in good faith."

Someone I loved. The words surged through Joe's mind as he tried to picture a grief-stricken Savanna. It was hard to do. Especially since she was always smiling and laughing as though she'd never endured a sad day in her life.

Joe couldn't stop himself from asking. "Who was he?"

She opened her eyes, but she didn't look at Joe. Instead, she stared at the toe of her white high heels as she answered, "My fiancé, Terry. He was in a car accident a month before we were to be married. His head was badly injured and for two weeks he slipped in and out of consciousness."

She paused to take a deep breath and Joe could see how much it was costing her to talk about her lost love. But he couldn't bring himself to tell her to stop. Something inside of him wanted to know her past, her pains, her hopes and dreams. Even though he knew it was wrong and risky, he wanted to know every private thing there was to know about Savanna.

"I stayed by his side as much as I could," she went on. "At times he was lucid and tried to talk. Mostly he wanted me to promise that I wouldn't waste my time grieving for him. That I would find another man to share my life with." She shook her head and smiled pensively. "I couldn't do that. At the time, it hurt too much. Maybe I should have lied just to make him feel better. But I don't know that I could have lived with that."

Suddenly Joe felt petty and selfish, and all the things in his life that had seemed so logical before didn't make nearly as much sense to him now. Dear God, what was happening to him? How could this woman be affecting him this way? He'd only known her a matter of days!

"Savanna," he said softly, "I'm sorry you had to go through that."

Her eyes held no regrets or grief as she lifted her face and gazed into his. "I'm sorry you lost your father, Joe. But he doesn't need you anymore. It's time to start living for yourself and for Megan."

"You make it all sound so simple."

Suddenly her melancholy mood was gone and a wide smile spread across her face. As Joe looked at her, his thoughts drifted back to last week when he'd danced with her in the darkness and her laughter had spilled over him like warm, sweet honey. He didn't know what it was, but she made him feel hope. Something he hadn't felt in a long, long time.

"It is, Joe. Just follow your heart."

Unwittingly he reached out and touched her smooth forehead, then slid his fingers down her cheeks until finally they were gently cradling her chin. "I'm not so sure I've got a heart anymore, Savanna."

Something dark and warm flared in her eyes as she lifted her hand and pressed her palm against his chest.

"It's there, Joe. You've just been ignoring it."

Maybe she was right, Joe thought. Because he could certainly feel the heavy thuds inside his chest beating faster and faster as he slid his hand down the deep V of her collar, until finally his fingers were resting against the cleft between her breasts.

"And what about your heart, Savanna? Is it still beating for your lost fiancé?"

The touch of his hand burned her skin, but it was the soft, yearning look on his face that was her complete undoing. "No," she whispered.

"Good. Because I don't want to kiss a woman who has another man on her mind."

"Joe—"

His name was all she could manage to say before his head bent to hers. "Be quiet, Savanna. You talk way too much."

The next instant his hands were on her shoulders drawing her into the tight circle of his arms and then his lips came down on hers, warm and totally consuming.

She shouldn't be doing this. The words were screaming in the back of her head. But her senses were too shocked, too overwhelmed by the taste, the smell and feel of him to do anything about it.

His mouth was slanting hungrily over hers, conveying a need to Savanna that transcended the physical. And she was drawn to that need. So much so that she wanted to give him everything he was asking for and more.

With a groan in her throat she stood on her tiptoes and curled her arms around his neck. Her eager response caused heat to flare through Joe's body. He forgot where they were as he spanned her waist with his hands and crushed her up against him.

His tongue thrust between her parted lips as his hands slipped up her back to where her skin was bared to his touch. She was like warm velvet, begging his fingers to stroke her, love her. And more than anything he wanted to do that. He wanted to go on kissing her forever. He wanted to hold on tight and never let her go.

As Joe's lips and hands explored and caressed her, a trembling started somewhere deep inside Savanna, then spread outward, until her legs were like sponges and her hands were clinging to his shoulders just to stay upright.

This was madness, her mind silently screamed. She had to get away from him before she lost her last shred of resistance and begged him to take her to his room and make slow, passionate love to her.

Wedging her hands between them, she pushed against his chest with all the strength she could muster. The unexpected movement caught Joe unaware and his grasp on her waist loosened. Savanna quickly tore her mouth from his and twisted out of his arms.

"Savanna! What—"

His unfinished question hung in the heavy night air as he watched her run back into the restaurant as though the devil himself was chasing her.

Dazed by what had just happened between them, Joe stared at the empty doorway for long moments. She was gone, he thought crazily. Just like that. One minute she'd been kissing him, turning him inside out, then the next she was gone. Damn it! What was she trying to do to him?

What are you trying to do to her? a voice inside him countered.

The question had him groaning and closing his eyes. Kissing Savanna had been a big mistake. Now that he knew how wonderful it was to have her in his arms, he wouldn't be able to look at her without wanting her.

Cursing under his breath, Joe pushed away from the balustrade and headed back into the hotel. It was going to be a long night, he realized. Long and lonely.

Chapter Eight

After a dreadful sleepless night, Savanna was up early the next morning, eager to get back to Oklahoma City and forget that last night she'd fallen into his arms like a lovesick teenager.

Savanna had thought about her behavior all night and she still couldn't figure out what had come over her. It was as if Joe had touched her and she'd instantly lost her senses.

She had to stop these silly notions that came into her head every time she looked at the man. Long ago she'd promised herself that she would never fall for another man. For five years now, she'd made it a point not to include a man in her future plans. And that's the way it was going to stay.

Joe McCann was mixed up. From what she could gather, he didn't even know what loving a woman was all about. But, oh, Lord, she thought as she lifted a brush to her hair, it had certainly felt as if he knew last night.

A knock sounded at her door. Savanna laid the brush aside and went to open it. Megan was standing out in the corridor, and the smile on her face was almost as bright as the striped short set she was wearing.

"Good morning, Savanna. Are you ready for breakfast?"

Actually, Savanna didn't think she could eat a thing, but considering she had to get on a plane later today, she knew she should put something into her stomach.

"Are you and your father ready?" she asked.

Megan nodded eagerly. "Daddy's waiting by the elevator. He sent me to fetch you."

A spurt of annoyance flashed through Savanna. Last night the man was kissing her as if he had every right as her lover, now he couldn't even come to her door and invite her to breakfast.

Well, what did you expect, Savanna? she asked herself dismally. The man is your boss. He didn't kiss you because he's fallen madly in love with you. He merely had a momentary lapse of sanity. And so had she!

"Just let me get my purse," she told Megan.

Seconds later she made sure the door was safely shut, then followed the teenager down the corridor to where Joe stood waiting.

As Savanna's eyes slid over him, she noticed he'd reverted back to his regular habits. In place of the business clothes he'd worn yesterday was a pair of blue jeans, black cowboy boots and a short-sleeved cotton shirt patterned in black and white. He'd looked professional and handsome yesterday. But Savanna preferred him dressed like this. Like the outdoor man he really was, not the suited businessman he pretended to be.

"Good morning, Joe," she murmured once they drew near him.

Joe nodded as his eyes flicked briefly over her green silk tank top and white slacks. This was the first time he'd seen

Savanna with her legs completely covered. Rather than dampening his interest, the slacks only fired his imagination even more.

"Good morning, Savanna," he drawled, his eyes lifting and connecting with her brown ones.

Her throat tightened and her heart took off in a foolish gallop. He looked so hard, so aloof. Yet everything inside of her wanted to put her arms around him and kiss him. She wanted to experience all the things she'd felt last night in his embrace.

"I hope you slept well," she said, feeling more awkward than she could ever remember feeling.

Joe turned away from her to punch the elevator button. "As well as ever," he replied. Which was the truth, Joe thought. He rarely slept well. Things were always on his mind. But never so much as they had been last night.

He was attracted to his secretary. No, he was more than attracted, he corrected himself. Last night he'd kissed her. Not like a friend. Not even like a lover. He'd kissed her as though she was his wife and he'd made love to her hundreds of times. And now, this very minute he wanted to do it all over again.

"I don't know about you two, but I'm starving," Megan spoke up. "May I have Belgian waffles for breakfast, Daddy?"

"You may have anything you want," Joe said as the elevator door opened and the three of them stepped inside.

"Gee," Megan said with cheery surprise. "That was easy. That business meeting you had yesterday must have put you in a generous mood."

Leonard Brown's promised thousands hadn't done it, Joe thought glumly. Savanna had. With a smile and a kiss she'd suddenly changed his world and he was afraid his life was never going to be the same again.

"Daddy, when are we going to catch a plane back to Oklahoma City?" Megan asked a few minutes later as she dug into whipped cream and crispy waffles.

Savanna looked up from her scrambled eggs and toast. She'd been wondering the same thing and hoping it would be this morning. She wanted to get home, visit with her friend Jenny and try to get her jumbled thoughts back in perspective. At least, that's what a part of her wanted. The crazy, reckless part of her wanted to spend as much time with Joe as she could.

Reaching for his coffee cup, Joe said, "Unfortunately, the first available flight back is not until seven thirty-five this evening. Everything else was booked full."

Seven thirty-five! That was hours and hours away, Savanna thought desperately.

"Wow, that's great!" Megan exclaimed.

Joe arched a brow at his daughter. "I fail to see the greatness of it. Sitting in an airport terminal for a day isn't my idea of having fun."

Fun? Since when had fun ever entered into any of Joe McCann's plans? Savanna wondered.

"Oh, no! We don't want to sit at the airport," Megan said with an emphatic shake of her head. "I've got a lot better idea. Let's drive down to Galveston and spend the day on the beach. It's not very far from here and I'll bet Savanna's never seen Galveston Island before, have you?"

The teenager turned an eager look on Savanna.

"No," Savanna conceded. "This is only the second time I've been in Texas. Most of my traveling has been done in the northern states."

Megan shot her father a triumphant look. "See, Daddy, you'd be doing something nice for Savanna. How can you say no?"

A week ago it wouldn't have been hard at all. He would have told his daughter to forget it, to pack her things and get ready to spend the afternoon in the airport. And he wouldn't have felt an ounce of guilt over it. But today he couldn't bring himself to disappoint his daughter or Savanna.

"We don't have a car, Megan," he said, but the excuse was only a halfhearted one and his daughter knew it.

Gulping down a mouthful of milk, she scooted excitedly to the edge of her seat. "We could rent one! And we could buy sandwiches and sodas and fruit for a picnic! Wouldn't you like that, Savanna?"

Before Savanna could respond, the teenager was shaking her head. "Oh, don't bother answering. I know you would," she told Savanna, then whirled her attention back to her father. "May we go, Daddy? It's been ages since we've done something fun."

"I didn't bring my swimming trunks," he said lamely.

Megan giggled a she whittled off another piece of waffle, then sopped it in whipped cream. "Yes, you did. I put them in with my things. Just in case," she added impishly. "And Savanna and I have our swimming suits with us."

Joe forced himself to look across the table at Savanna. She'd been surprisingly quiet through this whole thing and he could only wonder what had her so preoccupied. Maybe she was thinking she didn't want to go on a family outing with him and his daughter? But damn it, she was the one who'd been telling him he needed to loosen up and spend more recreational time with Megan.

"You haven't said anything, Savanna. What do you want to do?"

Savanna's eyes scanned his lean, masculine face. More than anything, she wanted to forget she'd ever kissed him. She wanted to deny that she was growing more and more attracted to him. But she couldn't. No more than she could say something that might knock Megan out of a day at the beach with her father. The girl needed that sort of time with her father. And as for Joe, well, he needed anything that would remind him there was life beyond McCann Drilling.

"It sounds like fun. I'd love to go," she agreed, then, finding it impossible to hold his gaze, she turned to Megan and gave the girl a smile.

Picking up his fork, Joe said, "Then I guess it's settled. We'll rent a car and drive to the beach."

"This is super! Really super! Can you believe it, Savanna? Daddy is really taking us to the beach."

Savanna smiled once again at the excited girl, then, lifting her coffee cup to her lips, she glanced over the rim at Joe. "Actually, I can't believe it. Has this Texas air done something to you?" she asked him.

To her amazement, a grin spread across his face. It crinkled the corners of his eyes and exposed his white teeth and gave Savanna a glimpse of the Joe she really wanted to know. And suddenly Savanna didn't care if she was living dangerously. To see him smile like this was almost worth risking her heart over.

"It's not the air, Savanna. I just decided I had a good day's work yesterday and deserved a little break. Besides, what man in his right mind could resist taking two beautiful women to the beach?"

"Oh, Daddy, you're flirting now," Megan said with a sly laugh. "I'll bet Savanna thinks you're awful."

No, Savanna thought, for once he was simply being a man. And she didn't know whether to be happy about that or run for her life.

"I think we'd better finish breakfast and get him down there quick before he changes his mind, Megan."

* * *

Galveston was about a fifty-mile drive down the interstate from Houston. On Megan's insistence Savanna sat in the front seat of the rental car with Joe, while she took the back.

"Have you ever seen anything like this?" Megan asked Savanna as the fingers of Galveston Bay began to appear to the left of them.

"Savanna said she lived in Seattle, Megan. That's by the Pacific Ocean and Puget Sound," Joe spoke up.

Surprised that he'd been paying that much attention, she glanced over at him. "So the geologist knows his geography," she teased. "So what bay was I living near when I lived in Boston?"

"Boston Bay," he said drolly. "And you had a redheaded boyfriend who chewed bubble gum all the time."

So he really had been listening. Savanna was both surprised and touched. Joe McCann wasn't a man who wasted his brain space on trivial things. Maybe he considered her a step above trivial. She liked that idea.

"Is that the only boyfriend you ever had Savanna?" Megan asked.

Savanna glanced at Joe, then back out the windshield. "No. I had a few others. My first serious love was when I was a senior in high school. We became engaged and were going to be married after graduation."

"That young!" Joe practically shouted. "Megan isn't even going to date until she's eighteen!"

"Daddy! That's crazy!"

Savanna looked over her shoulder and winked at Megan. To Joe she said, "So she's going to be able to choose who she wants for president before she's allowed to date a young man. That's rather strange logistics."

Joe grimaced. "If that's what it takes to keep Megan from getting into a bad relationship, then that's the way it has to be."

"Savanna looks like she's survived okay," Megan quickly countered. "What happened, anyway, Savanna? Did you get married?"

Savanna could feel Joe's eyes on her, but she didn't look his way. "No. We didn't get married. At the last minute he decided he wanted another girl more than he wanted me. So he left town with her and I was left with a wedding dress to get rid of."

"Oh," Megan groaned. "How awful for you. I'll bet you still hate him for that!"

Savanna laughed. "Actually, I'm grateful to him. He wouldn't have made a good husband and I was too young to be a wife."

A few moments passed, then Joe asked, "You were engaged twice?"

He sounded as though he found that incredible. Well, Savanna couldn't blame him. There weren't too many women her age with such a miserable record at losing fiancés.

A wry twist to her mouth, Savanna nodded. "That's right. I haven't exactly been lucky in love."

"What happened to the second guy?" Megan asked curiously. "Did he find another girl, too?"

"Savanna doesn't want to talk about that. Change the subject," he ordered Megan.

She shook her head at Joe. "I don't mind telling Megan. She's my friend." Glancing over her shoulder, she said, "My fiancé died from an accident, Megan."

The young girl's expression was suddenly contrite. "Oh, gee, I'm sorry, Savanna. That's too bad. I'll bet after all that, you probably don't ever want to get engaged again."

Savanna smiled wanly. ''No, getting engaged is the very last thing I'd want to do.''

Suddenly Galveston Bay came into view and the harbored ships caught Megan's attention. Scooting to the other end of the seat, she pressed her nose against the window for a better look.

''There's a giant oil tanker, Daddy. Do you think it might be carrying some of your oil?''

Joe glanced at the ship with the Texaco star painted on its side. *Do you want to be the new king of the American road?* Savanna's question drifted back to him, but surprisingly this time it didn't strike such a deep chord in him. He could honestly say he didn't want such lofty goals for himself. Joseph had wanted them for him. How could he ever forget that?

''I guess anything is possible,'' he told his daughter.

Less than an hour later they changed clothes, purchased food, drinks, beach towels and a tote bag to carry it all in, then loaded themselves back into the rental car and drove east on Highway 87 where the beach was more secluded.

Megan was the first one out of the car. She ran straight to the water, shrieking all the way. Laughing, Savanna raced after her, stripping off her cover-up as she went.

Back at the car, a smile touched Joe's mouth as he watched Savanna and his daughter splash their way into the warm surf of the gulf.

It didn't seem possible that only a week ago his daughter had been calling him twenty times a day, whining her discontent over the telephone, then crying her way through the evenings. Since Savanna had come to work for him, Megan hadn't shed one tear. She actually seemed glad to be living with him. As for Joe, having his daughter back with him had turned into something wonderful, like finding a piece of lost treasure.

He didn't want to admit it, but Savanna had done that for him. She wasn't just a secretary anymore. She was becoming a very real part of his life and he didn't see any way to stop it.

"Come on, Daddy, the water feels great!" Megan shouted.

"I'm coming," he called as he jogged down the grass-topped dunes, then across the warm, wet sand. "Don't chase away all the sharks. Leave one for me."

For the next hour they played in the salty waves. Much to Joe's surprise he discovered his daughter was a strong swimmer. So was Savanna. Several times he raced them both to shore. Though they never beat him, they stayed close on his heels.

Eventually all three waded ashore and spread the picnic out on a brightly striped beach towel. Savanna didn't think she'd be hungry after eating a large breakfast, but the exercise and fresh air had brought her appetite to life. She enjoyed every bite of the potato salad and cold fried chicken on her plate.

"I wish we could come back here for a vacation," Megan said wistfully. "Do you think we could? Sometime when you're not so busy with the company?"

Savanna set her can of soda aside and reached for a bottle of sunblock. As she rubbed it into her legs, she cut her gaze over to Joe, who was sitting to her left on the sand. She couldn't believe this was the same man who'd almost fired her for having a flat. He looked relaxed, almost happy.

Joe glanced over at his daughter. She looked like a typical, happy kid as she chewed on a chicken leg and dug her toes into the warm sand. He could see parts of himself in Megan. Her blue eyes, her stubborn dimpled chin and long gangly legs. Yet she was very unlike him when he'd been thirteen years old. But then, maybe Joe would've had his daughter's zest for living if Joseph had taken him to the beach once in a while. But Joseph hadn't taken him anywhere other than a rig site.

"Maybe we can this fall," he suggested. "Before school starts."

Well, that left her out of the picture, Savanna thought. Her job at McCann's would be over by then and she'd be out of their lives. The idea shouldn't make her feel sad. She had her career to think about. Whether Joe and his daughter went on a vacation or decided to stay home shouldn't matter to Savanna. But it did.

A few minutes later Megan finished her chicken, then left the two adults to hunt for shells on the beach. Once she was out of earshot, Savanna said, "Your daughter is enjoying herself."

Propping his arms on his raised knees, Joe turned his attention away from his daughter to Savanna. The stiff gulf breeze was whipping her hair, tousling her blond bangs away from her face. The saltwater had washed away her makeup. Yet she was beautiful barefaced, her brown eyes and fair skin glowing with life. Just looking at her made her feel good. "I hope this trip hasn't spoiled her. I don't want her to expect this sort of thing all the time."

"Give her a little credit, Joe. She's grown up enough to know life can't be a party seven days a week."

He sighed. "I don't know. You didn't see her the first few days after Deirdre had left her with me. She was either crying, whining or defiant."

Savanna recapped the bottle of sunblock and tossed it down by her bare feet. "I expect at that time she was feeling a little deserted by her mother and maybe even a bit afraid of you."

His expression turned incredulous. "Afraid of me? Why, I've never laid a harsh hand on her! There wouldn't be any reason for her to be afraid of her own father!"

Resting her cheek on her knee, she looked at him. "From what you told me, you and Megan had spent very little time together. She didn't know what to expect from you, or what kind of life she was going to have with you as her parent. That's enough to make any little girl afraid."

He grimaced. "If that was the case, I think she's gotten over it. At least, she seems to have changed for the better."

Savanna laughed softly, and the sound drew his eyes to her lips. All day he'd relived their kiss in his mind, and now as he looked at the full, smooth texture of her lips he wanted more than anything to bend his head and taste them again.

Doing his best to shake away the thought, he asked, "Why are you laughing?"

"Because…well, Megan would probably say that you've changed."

Had he? Joe asked himself. He didn't think so. He was still Joe McCann, owner of McCann Drilling. He was still Joseph's son. Maybe he had taken time off today to relax on the beach, but that didn't mean his priorities had changed. Tomorrow he'd be back in the office, trying his best to make McCann's the success it once was. That's the way it had to be. The way it would always be. If he could just get Savanna out of his head.

"Just because I let Megan talk me into this beach thing doesn't mean I'm getting soft," he said, his voice a little gruff.

Savanna laughed again. "I can't see you getting soft over anything," she told him, then stretched out on her back.

Thankfully, clouds had gathered earlier in the day, blocking out most of the blistering rays. Crossing her arms behind her head, she closed her eyes and breathed in the salty, damp breeze.

From the moment Savanna had stripped off her cover-up Joe had been trying his best not to notice her body. But he was failing miserably. With her lying beside him on the sand, it was impossible not to let his eyes glide over her smooth skin and ripe curves.

Her swimming suit was deep teal green and although it was one piece, it was far from modest. The legs were cut up high on her hips, while the neckline dipped deeply between her breasts. Joe swallowed convulsively as his eyes rested on the faint outline of her nipples beneath the stretchy fabric.

"Joe?"

"Hmmm?"

She opened her eyes to find him staring at her, his eyes narrowed against the wind and glare. He was a handsome man. She'd thought that many times before. Even the very first time she'd seen him. But today she was seeing more than just the pleasing, masculine lines of his face, the striking blue of his eyes and thick tawny wave of hair falling over his forehead. She was seeing a softer, gentler side of him and it drew her to him in a way that nothing had yet.

"What did you do when you were a kid?"

Frowning, he reached for a bag of chocolate cookies. "What do you mean? I guess I did what most every kid does. I went to school."

"Did you play sports?"

He shrugged and pulled a cookie from the bag. "Very little."

"Why very little? You look like you would have made a perfect baseball player."

Funny that Savanna should say that. Every spring and summer he'd yearned to play baseball, but he'd never gotten to join in with the other boys. He'd either been studying science or accompanying his father to potential rig sites. He'd never got the chance to find out if he could catch a line drive or hit a home run. But he'd learned all about drilling for petroleum.

"I didn't have time for baseball. I had other things to do."

"Other things to do?" she asked. "What sort of things? You mean things like riding bikes, fishing in the creek or running a paper route?"

Suddenly he was laughing, but to Savanna disappointment the sound was full of bitterness.

"Joseph McCann would never have allowed his son to run a paper route. That sort of thing was for poor kids. Besides, I was always in training."

Intrigued by his strange confession, Savanna turned on her side and propped her head on her palm. "That's the weirdest thing I've ever heard. What sort of training were you doing?"

He bit into the cookie, then, looking out to where Megan played at the water's edge, he said, "Training to be an oilman. What else?"

Savanna shook her head. "Joe, I'm not talking about when you were an older teenager. I meant when you were younger, like eight, nine and twelve. You couldn't have been training to be an oilman then," she argued.

With a snort he popped the rest of the cookie into his mouth. "You didn't know my father, Savanna. From the time I was old enough to understand that oil came out of the ground and gasoline was made from that oil...well, that was it. My life was planned for me."

Savanna was stunned. "But that's—it's unbelievable. Didn't you ever speak up? Tell your father what you wanted?"

He shrugged as though that part of his life hadn't really affected him that much, but the bitterness Savanna saw in his eyes told her otherwise.

"No one told Joseph McCann anything. They listened." He shifted around on the sand so that he was facing her. "Anyway," he went on, "I honestly did like science, so spending my summers at science camp really wasn't all that bad."

"What did your mother think about all this?"

"She didn't like it. Mother resented all the time and money Joseph spent on the company. She wanted other, simpler things for me. But she never had that much influence with her husband and finally she gave up trying."

Savanna had always thought of her childhood as being difficult. She'd never had a permanent home, or friends that she could pal with for more than six months at a time. But compared to Joe's, her adolescent years had been wonderful.

"I don't understand, Joe. What about all those things I talked about? Like riding bikes, fishing, playing baseball. Didn't you want to do those things?"

He turned his head to look down the beach at Megan. Savanna watched the wind lift and play with his hair, before her gaze slipped downward to glide slowly over his roughly hewn profile. She'd been wrong about Joe all along, she thought sadly. He wasn't a man who'd forgotten how to laugh and love. He was a man who'd never learned how.

"Of course I wanted to do those things," he answered as he turned his eyes back on Savanna. "But I couldn't refuse my father. Perhaps Megan wasn't so far off the other night when she likened her grandfather to J. R. Ewing. He was flamboyant, successful, simply larger than life. Everything he touched turned to money. And he'd achieved all that without a high school diploma. To me, he was almost god-like and I would have done anything to please him. Even give up my whole childhood.''

And he was still giving up for his father, she concluded. Could he not see that? Or was that the way he wanted it to be?

"Did you ever think your father might be wrong about things?" she asked after a few moments had passed.

Joe never talked to anyone about his relationship with his father. Even his mother had stopped broaching the subject because that's the way Joe wanted it. But it was different with Savanna. He wanted to tell her these things. He wanted her to understand why he felt so compelled to push himself to succeed in his father's footsteps.

"Oh yeah. Many times. Like Megan mentioned, I had my rebellious streaks at times. I married Deirdre despite my father's warnings. The marriage didn't last. Then when my father started pulling me out of the field and putting me behind a desk, I quit and went to work for Red Man Oil Company as their head exploration man."

"Was he furious over that?" Savanna asked.

He let out a mocking snort. "Furious? No. Joseph McCann didn't get furious over anything. He was too confident for that. He knew I'd be back and he was right. Two years later Red Man folded and I was forced to go back to McCann's." He chuckled, but it was a hard, cynical sound, full of self-recriminations.

"It's like the old television show, Savanna. Father knows best."

Savanna sat up and reached for his hands. He gave them to her and she curled her fingers firmly around his. "You didn't cause Red Man to fold, did you?"

He shook his head. "No, it went under because of a bad business decision. But I can't put the blame for my broken marriage on someone else."

"Maybe not. But if Joseph McCann had left you alone and allowed you to grow and be your own man, you and your marriage would have been a lot happier. Can't you see that?"

Joe had never thought so before. And he didn't want to think so now. He liked to believe he was a strong man. Strong enough to accept the blame for his failures. Maybe Joseph had demanded a lot from him, and maybe he hadn't been a normal father, but he'd loved him in his own way. And in the end that's all Joe had ever really wanted from him. Simply to be loved.

Tightening his hold on her hands, he stood, drawing Savanna to her feet along with him. "You know," he said gently, "you're like that blonde in the musical *South Pacific*. A cockeyed optimist."

A smile spread across her face. He was beginning to know her after all. "I believe that's the nicest thing you've said to me."

A grin lifted one corner of his mouth. "I can be nice. Sometimes. When the mood hits me."

And what sort of mood was hitting him now? Savanna wondered as her brown eyes met his. There was something provocative, even daring in the look he was giving her, and every cell in her body responded to it.

Leaning closer, she touched her fingers to his cheek, his chin and finally his bottom lip. "I think you can be more than nice, Joe McCann. I think you can be anything you want to be. If you want it badly enough," she murmured.

At this moment there was no doubt in Joe's mind as to what he wanted. He wanted Savanna. In some secluded place, her arms around his neck, her bare, warm body pressed against his. He wanted to taste her lips until he was drunk on their sweetness, he wanted to fill himself with her joy and laughter. He wanted to make love to her. The kind of passionate love that made the sky dip down to touch the earth.

But they weren't alone, he silently argued with himself. And even if they were, he couldn't lose his head and make the same sort of mistake with Savanna that he had with Deirdre. No, he thought grimly. His heart just wasn't capable of handling that sort of pain again.

Breathing in deeply, he drew her hand from his face and held it tightly against his chest. "You're a tempting woman, Savanna. In more ways than one."

Suddenly Savanna's heart was beating in her throat. Joe wasn't her boss anymore. He was a hot-blooded male and she was in imminent danger of getting scorched.

"Well, that's a lot better than being nosy," she said with a breathless laugh, then tugged on his hand. "Let's go look for shells. We might find one to take back with us. So then when we look at it, we'll remember this trip."

Joe allowed her to lead him toward the wet strip of beach in front of them. Sea gulls screeched above their heads and strutted across the sand. Savanna's hand was warm and soft, her fingers curled invitingly around his. In the distance his daughter was waving happily at them.

He wouldn't need a shell to remind him of this trip, he realized. This was a day he would never forget.

Chapter Nine

Savanna shifted her shopping bag to the other arm and followed her friend Jenny across the mall to a small dress shop.

"I don't know why I agreed to come to the mall with you tonight," the redhead said. "I don't need a thing. But when I get in here all I want to do is spend money."

Savanna stood beside her friend as she peered into the plate glass at a silk broomstick skirt. "I don't like to shop by myself," she explained. "And I didn't have a pair of panty hose left without a run."

"You could have worn slacks to work tomorrow," Jenny suggested.

Savanna supposed that would have been the easy thing to do instead of driving halfway across the city to the mall. But she'd been unusually restless all day, and coming home to her empty apartment this evening hadn't helped matters. The need for panty hose had given her a good excuse to get Jenny to go out shopping.

"It's too hot for slacks," Savanna reasoned.

"Just wait until July and August. It gets as hot as a fire-cracker in this part of the country. Think you'll still want to hang around?"

Jenny turned away from the window and the two women moved slowly away from the dress and on down the wide, busy corridor of the mall.

"I'm positive," Savanna assured her. "But I think I'm going to need a car with air conditioner. My dress was wet by the time I made it to work this morning."

"Speaking of work," Jenny said as she bumped into Savanna in order to miss a group of giggling teenaged girls. "I'm ready to hear all about your trip. How did it go?"

Savanna shrugged, but inwardly she was feeling anything but nonchalant. While they'd been away, something had happened between her and Joe. And it went beyond the kiss they'd shared on the hotel balcony.

Today at work nothing had seemed the same. Each time she'd looked at Joe she'd wanted to go to him, touch him, talk to him about things that had nothing to do with the letters she was typing or the entries she'd made into the ledger.

"It was successful. Joe agreed to sign a contract to drill two new wells in the Southeastern part of the state."

Jenny made an impatient sound. "I'm not talking about business. I'm talking about you and him. Did anything happen between the two of you?"

Savanna groaned. "Jenny, I told you before, Joe's got other things on his mind besides women."

Jenny paused beside a display of shoes outside a shoe store. Picking up a pair of leather sandals, she said thoughtfully, "Then I guess you had a boring business trip."

Savanna couldn't prevent the flush of heat coloring her cheeks. "Well, we did drive down to Galveston Island before we flew home. His daughter wanted to visit the beach."

Jenny looked at her with raised brows. "Well, now," she said suggestively, "if my sergeant took me to Galveston Island, I'd think he other things on his mind than talking police work."

Savanna could feel the blush on her face deepen. "It wasn't like that. Megan was with us."

"And if she hadn't been?"

"Jenny!" Savanna gasped. "There's nothing between me and my boss." Nothing but a kiss that had been burned into her mind forever, she thought desperately.

Jenny dropped the sandals back onto the rack and picked up a pair of red high heels. "That's too bad," she said as she looked at the price tag.

"Too high?" Savanna asked.

Jenny laughed. "No, silly. About you and Joe, the oilman. I'd like to see you find a man. And he sounds like a good one."

"Jenny, I've told you how disastrous my engagements turned out to be. Do you think I'd be idiotic enough to try again? Besides," she went on in a calmer tone, "I want to be a CPA. Not a wife. And Joe, well, even if he were interested in me, he's just too complicated for my taste."

"Honey," Jenny said with a laugh, "all men are complicated. They're born that way."

Savanna frowned at her friend. "I can't believe you, of all people, want me to get involved with a man. You hate men!"

Jenny kicked off her loafer and jammed her foot into the red high heel. "I don't hate men. I just don't trust them. Especially where I'm concerned. But you're different.

You're young and beautiful and all heart. You should have a husband and babies.''

Savanna thought Jenny should have the same thing for herself. But she didn't say so. She knew her friend had been hurt badly by her ex-husband, not just emotionally but physically, too. She didn't want to say anything that might bring all that pain back to her.

''Maybe I will have all that someday,'' Savanna said, her voice unknowingly wistful. ''But right now I plan to be a career woman. Books and numbers. That's going to be my life.''

Jenny tilted her foot first one way and then the other. ''What do you think?''

''About what?'' Savanna asked as she stared absently out at the passing shoppers.

''The high heels. Think I should buy them?''

Savanna looked down at Jenny's feet. ''They're definitely dressy. Where would you wear them?''

''I don't know. But they look good. What more reason do I need to buy them?'' she asked with a laugh.

''I can't think of any,'' Savanna said, doing her best to laugh along with her friend.

But once Jenny went inside the store to pay for the shoes, the smile fell from Savanna's face. For the first time in a long time she wasn't in the mood for laughing. She was troubled and confused.

All she could think about was Joe. The things he'd told her about his childhood, the way he'd looked at her on the beach, the way he'd kissed her on the balcony. He was beginning to consume her every waking thought and she didn't know what to do about it.

But she had to do something, she fiercely told herself. Joe was her boss. She couldn't let herself get hung up on him.

"Okay, there went a day's wages," Jenny said when she rejoined Savanna. "What do you say we go get some ice cream, then head back home. I've got to go on patrol at nine tonight and it's nearly eight now."

"I'm always ready for ice cream," Savanna assured her. But she definitely wasn't ready to lose her heart to Joe McCann.

The next day at work, Joe was away from the office until midafternoon. When he eventually returned he immediately got on the telephone and stayed there for nearly a half hour. As soon as he hung up, he poured himself a cup of coffee and carried it over to Savanna's desk.

She looked up at him, her heart pounding foolishly, her eyes happy to be seeing him again. "Did you want something?"

Joe came close to laughing. Hell, he thought, he wanted lots of things. Her most of all. He could admit that now. But wanting was all he intended to let himself do.

"I, uh, have something I wanted to talk to you about," he said.

The grim expression on his face had her eyes widening with concern. "Oh, have I done something wrong?"

Yeah, he thought, his eyes sliding over her. She'd come to work looking entirely too beautiful. She was wearing a dress printed with big pink roses. It buttoned all the way down the front and exposed her thigh when she walked or crossed her legs. Joe felt a little short of breath every time he looked at her.

"No. It's nothing like that." He took a deep breath as his eyes left her crossed legs and settled to her lips. They were dark pink, moist and parted with anticipation. The sight of them had him groaning inside.

For the past two days since they'd returned from Houston all Joe had been able to think about was Savanna and how incredible it had felt to kiss her. Looking at her now, he wanted nothing more than to lock the door, unbutton those roses and explore every inch of her.

Drawing in another long breath, he sat on the edge of the desk. "I've got to go out of town again."

"Back to Houston?" she asked, while thinking her resistance would never be able to survive another trip with him.

Joe shook his head. "No. The excavation for one of the rig sites is nearly completed. I want to be there while the rat holes are being started."

"Rat holes?"

He nodded. "Before large drilling pipe can be used, a starting hole has to be bored and filled with casing. We oilman call that ratholing."

"I see," Savanna said. "How long will you be gone?"

His eyes on the toes of his boots, he said, "It depends on the weather and how much the crew can get done. Three days, more than likely."

Savanna felt totally deflated. "And the office?"

"I'll give you the keys. Just open at the same time in the mornings and keep doing the things you've been doing. Of course, I'll have a cellular phone with me in case a problem arises here that you can't handle."

She nodded, then realizing he still wasn't looking at her, she said, "I'll do my best."

Long moments passed. When he didn't make a move to leave her desk, she asked, "Was there anything else you needed to tell me?"

Joe set his coffee cup on the desk by his hip, then rubbed his hand against the back of his neck. "Actually, there is. I haven't yet decided what to do about Megan."

A few days ago he'd more or less blasted her for trying to give him advice about Megan. Now he was asking? She couldn't believe it. "You're not planning on taking her with you?" she asked.

He turned his head to look at her. "No. It's too remote. I'll be bunking with some of the crew and there wouldn't be any place for her to stay. Besides, I doubt I'll have a minute to spare while I'm down there."

"I see. Do you have someone to stay with her?"

"That's what I've been thinking about. I have a neighbor who's a widow and probably wouldn't mind watching over Megan for a couple of days. You think that would be suitable?"

A thoughtful frown creased Savanna's face. "Has Megan met her?"

"No. But Mrs. Grady is a nice woman. Megan should be able to get along with her. If you don't think that's a good idea, I have a friend over in Mustang that would be glad to keep her. He and his wife have three small children. They know all about kids."

They probably did, Savanna thought. But the girl was just now getting adjusted to a new home and a father she'd never lived with before. She didn't need to be thrown among total strangers for the next couple of days. It would be asking too much of Megan.

Savanna rose to her feet, bringing her face level to his. "I think I should stay with Megan," she stated.

He stared at her as though her suggestion was the very last thing he'd consider. "*You* stay with her?"

Savanna shrugged and tried her best to appear casual. But that was hard to do when her heart was pounding, waiting for his response.

"Why not?" she countered.

A frown creasing his face, he looked away from her. "Because you're my secretary. Not Megan's baby-sitter."

Though they shouldn't have, his words cut her. She'd thought in the past days she'd become more to him than just a secretary. The kiss they'd shared had certainly left her feeling like more than just his employee. But maybe that kiss and the time they'd spent on the beach hadn't really meant anything to him.

"I could be both," she suggested quietly.

"No. I don't think that would be wise, Savanna," he said bluntly.

Her brown eyes flashed with annoyance. So now he was back to being Mr. Cool, she thought. Well, if that's what he really wanted, then so be it. But she wasn't about to make it easy for him.

"Why?" she asked, in a voice as curt as his.

Joe groaned inwardly. Damn it, didn't she know why? He was already getting too close, too attached to Savanna. Asking her to stay in his home with his daughter would be as foolish as striking a match near a puddle of gasoline. An explosion of some sort was bound to happen.

But when she was standing close to him like this, her flowery fragrance filling his head, it was hard to hold on to his common sense, much less keep his hands off her.

"I think you know the answer to that, Savanna."

"Because you don't think it would be proper?" she retorted, then groaned with frustration. "Joe, do you always have to be so ramrod straight? Can't you ever let your hair down and quit worrying about every little decision you make? Does everything in your life have to be precise and planned?"

Savanna stood watching him, waiting for a reply. But her answer didn't come in words. She read it on his face. He wanted her physically. And that was making him afraid to let her into his home and near his daughter.

Her heart pounding wildly, she said, "Joe, just because we kissed doesn't mean—"

Before she could finish, he caught her by the shoulders and tugged her around the corner of the desk to where he sat.

"We did more than kiss, Savanna!" he hissed, just inches away from her face. "And you know it! What are you trying to do to me, anyway? Tempt me any way you can, just so you can see how much it will take to make me crumble?"

"You're crazy! Just because I want to watch out for Megan doesn't mean I'm trying to seduce you!" she said, her voice rising, her breast heaving with anger. "I told you I don't want *any* man. And that includes *you!*"

"Liar," he growled, jerking her between his thighs and up against his chest. "I'm going to prove you wrong right here and now!"

"Joe—"

Once again, his name was all she managed to get out before his lips came down over hers. Moaning, Savanna squirmed and tried to twist free of his grasp. But his hands came up to catch both sides of her face in a viselike grip, making it impossible for her to avoid his kiss.

Then suddenly the warm, male taste of him began to weave its magic over her and Savanna didn't care if she ever got away. She had been lying when she'd said she didn't want him. She wanted him with a vengeance that had kept her awake the past two nights. Now that he was giving her just what she'd been aching for, she couldn't resist him.

Feeling the response of her lips against his, Joe eased his hold on her face to find the buttons on the front of her dress. He released the first two, then lifted his head to look at her.

"Are you going to deny you want me?" he asked huskily.

How could she? Savanna wondered miserably. At this moment she wanted him more than anything she'd ever wanted in her life.

"No," she whispered. "Are you going to say you don't really want me? That this is just some sort of test to get the truth out of me?"

Sliding his fingers beneath the loosened neckline of her dress, he said, "I've wanted you from the moment you walked in that door, Savanna Starr. Does that make you happy?"

No, she thought. Nothing would make her happy now. Except him. Him touching her, kissing her, loving her until they were both so out of their minds they couldn't think about tomorrow.

Rather than tell him with words, she raised on tiptoes and brought her lips up to his.

Joe didn't need any further encouragement. With a heated groan his mouth took hers in a deep, hungry kiss. Beneath the fabric of her dress his hand slid downward until he reached her lace-covered breast.

Pressing the lower half of her body closer to his, Savanna parted her lips. The silent invitation had Joe thrusting his tongue into the dark, sweet recesses of her mouth. At the same time his fingers worked frantically to loosen the remaining buttons on her dress.

When the fabric finally fell away, his hands plunged inside the cups of her bra then lifted her breasts free of the confining lace. The moment their softness spilled into his hands, Joe dropped his head and tasted one pink nipple and then the other.

Groaning with reckless abandon, Savanna tangled her fingers in his tawny hair and anchored his head to her breast. Never in her life had she needed anything the way she needed Joe at this moment. Couldn't he feel it? Didn't he know that no man had ever touched her like this? Made her ache like this?

"Dear God, Savanna, it's crazy what you do to me!"

His voice was oddly tight as though he was forcing the words through a fog of desire. The sound was strangely inciting to Savanna and she drew his hands up to her breasts and held them there.

"Kiss me, Joe," she whispered against his lips.

She didn't have to ask him again. Joe was tired of thinking, worrying, weighing the consequences of his actions. He wanted Savanna with every fiber of his being, and she wanted him. He wasn't going to let himself think beyond that. For once in his life, he was simply going to feel.

"I don't know what it is about you, Savanna," he whispered, "but you make me forget every rule in the book."

Bringing her hands up to his face, she urged him closer. "Then I must be doing something right."

Joe closed the fraction of space between their lips. Oh, yes, she was doing everything right, he thought. So right that he never wanted this moment in her arms to end.

Groaning with a need that went beyond the physical, Joe tasted her mouth, her cheeks, her chin, then slowly trailed his lips down her arched throat. By the time he reached the mound of her breast, Savanna was panting short little breaths of anticipation and so lost to him that when the telephone shrilled loudly she dazedly looked over her shoulder at the ringing instrument, then back to Joe.

"Do you want me to answer that?"

He wanted to jerk the line out of the wall. But it was too late for that now. Cursing under his breath, he snatched the receiver off the hook. "McCann Drilling," he said hoarsely.

Long minutes passed as he listened to the person at the other end of the line. After a while it became obvious to Savanna that the call was something he couldn't put off and their moment of passion had ended.

Walking some distance from him, she turned her back and refastened her clothing. Dear Lord, she silently groaned as she fingered the button between her breasts. She'd nearly made love to Joe! In the middle of the afternoon. In his office, for Pete's sake! What was wrong with her?

With her palms pressed against her hot cheeks, Savanna closed her eyes and breathed in deeply. But the extra oxygen didn't seem to help. The aching in her body had seeped into her heart and she was shaking all over with the enormity of what that meant.

She loved Joe McCann. She wanted to give him more than her body. She wanted to give him her heart, her love, every part of herself.

Galvanized by the sudden realization, Savanna turned and hurried past Joe and out the door. Down the corridor in the bathroom, she braced both hands on the edge of the lavatory and let her head drop until her chin hit her chest.

What was she going to do? What could she do? Joe might want her sexually, but he didn't want a wife. And she didn't want to tangle her heart up with a man. Especially one who didn't even like himself, much less her.

Lifting her head, she gazed at her reflection in the mirror. Stunned by what she saw, Savanna lifted her fingers and touched them to her bare, puffed lips. Who was this woman with mussed hair, wide dark eyes and a very kissed mouth? she asked herself. Was this the same woman who had vowed never to risk her heart by loving another man?

No. It wasn't the same woman, she realized. Because the Savanna that had suffered through the humiliation of desertion and grieved over Terry's death hadn't really known what loving a man was all about.

A few minutes ago Joe had taken her on a magical trip, a place where only true lovers could go, a place she'd never been before. Now she was desperately afraid she was going to find out what it was really like to love and lose.

A few minutes later, when Savanna returned to the office, Joe was hanging up the telephone. She shut the door behind her, then stood motionless.

Rebuttoning the blue denim shirt she'd torn open, he walked toward her, his gaze scanning her face. "Are you all right?"

She wanted to run to him, press her cheek against his chest and simply hold on to him. Instead, she swallowed at the tightness in her throat and nodded.

Once he reached her, his fist came up beneath her chin and he rubbed his knuckles ever so gently against her jawline.

"I don't know what to say to you, Savanna," he said in a low voice. "I don't know whether I'm sorry things between us got out of hand, or if I'm sorry because we didn't get to finish what we started."

Even now, the simple touch of his hand was enough to make her heart pound with longing. "Maybe we'd better forget it ever happened," she murmured.

A few moments ago, before she'd returned to the office, he'd thought the same thing, but seeing her now made him realize how foolish that idea was.

His eyes dropped to the thrust of her breasts, then his hand quickly followed to trace a forefinger along the open neckline of her dress. "I don't think that will be possible, Savanna."

In fact, Joe was certain he'd never be able to forget the fire she'd built inside him, the exquisite pleasure she'd given him for those few minutes.

"I don't want to make love to you, Joe," she said, her voice as shaky as her hands.

A wry grin cocked his mouth. "Then you're a damn good actress, Savanna."

She closed her eyes and wondered if her heart would ever get back to a normal pace. "That's not what I meant."

"What do you mean?" he asked, then, unable to resist, he leaned forward and pressed his lips against the side of her neck.

Moaning, she reached for the sides of his waist. "Don't do this, Joe," she pleaded breathlessly. "Don't tempt me to have sex with you. I don't ever intend to give myself to any man, unless I marry him. And we both certainly know you don't want that."

Like a dash of cold water, her words sobered him. He pulled back from her and looked into her eyes. "You mean . . . are you suggesting that you're a virgin?"

Hearing him say it caused a flush of embarrassment to wash over her face. "I know you think that's prudish, but I've been through too much in the past to simply give myself away now."

His expression turned incredulous. "A few minutes ago you were willing to give me anything. You weren't too worried about your virginity then."

The color receded from her face to leave her cheeks deathly pale. "A few minutes ago I was out of my mind. And so were you," she added.

His features suddenly grim, he lifted his arms to either side of her head and planted her to the door. "If you'll do a little thinking, Savanna, you'll remember that you're the one who's been telling me I need to loosen up, quit living my life by the rules. What's the matter now? You don't like me this way?''

She loved him this way! Every way! Damn it, couldn't he see that?

"You just want sex, Joe. And I... Well, after that phone rang and I—'' she stopped and drew in a bracing breath "—could think, I realized that I needed more than that.''

Joe wanted to be annoyed with her. He wanted to say to hell with her starched ideas. But he couldn't. The anguish in her eyes, the quivering of her lips touched him, turned his insides as soft as butter.

"Maybe I need more, too, Savanna. But I—'' Shaking his head he dropped his arms and stepped back from her. "I've got to go. I've got some wells to drill.''

Her eyes searched his. "What—about Megan?''

Turning, he picked up a hard hat and jammed it on his head. "Do you really want to stay with her?''

Maybe Joe was right, Savanna silently reasoned. Maybe it wouldn't be wise to insert herself into his home and the life of his daughter. But Megan needed her. And what could it hurt now? She'd already committed the mistake of falling in love with him.

"Megan feels comfortable with me and I don't like to think of her having to stay with strangers.''

He tucked his shirt into his blue jeans. Just watching him made Savanna weak in the knees. She'd come so close to making love to him. She still wanted to make love to him! But what she wanted and needed were two entirely different things. She had to remember that.

"Then stay with her,'' he said, his voice sounding suddenly drained. "I'll be leaving in the morning. She'll be all right with Ophelia until you get off work tomorrow evening.''

"Thank you, Joe.''

He slanted her a wry look. "For what? Answering the phone and saving you from my clutches?"

Her heart felt sick and she wasn't even sure why. She only knew that she wanted Joe in a way that he would never want her.

"No," she said quietly. "For allowing me to stay with your daughter. She's come to mean a lot to me."

And Savanna had come to mean a lot to him, Joe realized. He hadn't meant it to turn out that way. She'd walked into this office a complete stranger, just a replacement for Edie. And that's all he'd planned for her to be. But now he couldn't imagine this place without her. He couldn't imagine himself without her.

"I'll tell her tonight that you'll be coming tomorrow after work."

She nodded and he turned and opened the door. Before he walked through it, he glanced over his shoulder at her. "I'll be out in the work yard...if you need me."

Was he being deliberately suggestive? In spite of everything, the idea of Joe doing something like flirting put a smile on her face. "If I do, I'll find you."

He reached out and ruffled the top of her blond hair. "Well, if you have to come looking, don't forget to wear a hard hat. I don't want anything falling on this head of yours."

The soft look of concern in his eyes went straight to Savanna's heart and for one wild moment she considered taking him by the hand, tugging him back into the office and locking the door behind them. But she couldn't. She'd made her choice long ago, the day she'd watched Terry being lowered into the cold ground.

"Don't worry. I don't plan on taking a risk." Not for anyone, or anything, she thought sadly.

He nodded, then turned and went on down the corridor. Savanna watched him until he was totally out of sight before she shut the door and walked over to a pile of pens scattered on the floor in front of Joe's desk.

Squatting on her heels, she gathered them back into a small tin replica of an oilcan. By the time she placed it on the corner of his desk, tears were falling from her eyes.

Chapter Ten

"This is my very best dive, Savanna. I could do it when I was six years old," Megan said with proud accomplishment.

Savanna pushed her sunglasses up on her forehead to see Megan standing on the edge of the swaying diving board. "Okay, I can see you better now. Go for it," she urged the teenager.

Megan bounced once, twice, then sent her slim body arcing through the air in a tight somersault. At the last minute her arms and legs straightened and she entered the water with hardly a splash.

Savanna was applauding when Megan's head bobbed above the surface of the water.

"That was great, honey! You looked like an Olympic star!" Savanna exclaimed.

A happy smile on her face, Megan climbed out of the pool and came over to where Savanna sat on the patio.

"Do you really think so?" the teen asked.

"I certainly do. Does your father know you have a talent for diving?" Savanna asked her.

Megan shook her head. "No," she answered glumly. "He's never been too interested in sports."

"Well, perhaps you should tell him how much you like it, anyway. He might surprise you and let you take more lessons."

Frowning, Megan reached for a towel and swiped it down her long legs. "I doubt it. He only thinks academics are important."

How sad, Savanna thought, that Joe had grown up to be just like Joseph, who'd thought science and learning to be an oilman was the only thing his young son had needed in his life.

She reached for a glass of lemonade sitting on a nearby table. After taking a long sip, Savanna glanced thoughtfully at Megan. "I think you have to agree that your dad seems to be relaxing about a few things."

Megan tilted her head to one side as she contemplated Savanna's words. "Well, he has been different here lately. Ever since you came to work for him. I think he likes you. A lot."

Savanna slid her sunglasses back on her nose. Oh, yes, she thought wryly as memories of the heated moments they'd shared yesterday in the office swept through her mind. Joe liked the physical parts of her, all right.

"I don't know about that. But he's just now learning how to be a daddy, Megan. It might take him a while to get the hang of it."

Smiling, Megan sank down beside Savanna's chair, wound her arm through hers and gave it an affectionate squeeze. "Well, I can be patient with Daddy as long as you're around, Savanna," she said, then her expression turned serious as another thought hit her. "You—you're not going to leave, are you?"

"Leave?" Savanna asked with surprise. "You mean like leave town?"

Her face a picture of worry, Megan nodded.

Savanna knew exactly what was going through Megan's mind, and her heart went out to her. So many times, Savanna had wanted to be reassured that nothing would change in her life, that her home would always be in the same place, her friends would remain the same and her parents would never leave her for any reason.

Smiling gently, Savanna patted Megan's damp cheek. "No, honey. I'm not going to leave. Oklahoma City is my home now."

"Good," the girl said with a huge sigh of relief. "'Cause I don't want you to leave. Ever."

Ever. Savanna didn't think Joe would want her hanging around for that long.

Joe stood with his boots ankle-deep in mud and his shirt sopped with rain as he waited for the bulldozer to come to a halt. As soon as it did, he strode angrily over to the piece of heavy equipment and climbed up on the track.

"I don't know who the hell decided the reserve pit was supposed to be here. Whoever it was I'd like to get my hands on them!" Joe shouted over the idling motor.

The operator shook his head. "It wasn't me, Mr. Mc-Cann. I just push where they tell me to push."

"Well, this will never work. Fill this damn hole up and don't do anything else until I tell you!"

The burly operator shrugged his shoulders. "Whatever you say, boss," he said, then throttled up the engine to a loud roar.

Joe jumped down from the tracks and dismissed the driver with a wave of his hand. Then he turned and walked across fifty yards of sludge to a blue-and-white doghouse.

Three men were inside the small metal workroom, sitting on a bench lined against one wall. A gas lantern sat on the floor at one end, shedding precious little light against the black, rainy weather.

"Hey, boss." The youngest of the three spoke up. "We just ate lunch. But we might have a sandwich or two left if you want one."

Joe glanced at his watch. It was six o'clock in the evening, but the men were just now eating lunch. Even though he didn't ask or demand it, they gave him 200 percent of themselves. At times like this, his crew's loyalty made him feel guilty, made him wonder if they didn't deserve a better boss, who could make McCann more productive, one who could double their wages instead of barely meeting payroll, a boss like his father.

"Thanks, Robert, but I'll get something to eat later."

"Have you ever seen rain like this?" one of the other men asked.

Joe pulled off his hard hat and wiped a handkerchief over his face. "I've never seen *anything* like this, period," he muttered. "And I don't mean this damn rain."

The three workmen exchanged anxious glances, then the oldest, who was the foreman of the crew, asked, "What's the matter?"

Joe wiped a hand through his damp hair. "I hate to tell you this, Mac, but this rat hole needs to be moved a good thirty yards to the north."

"What! The men have worked their butts off on the hole. Now we've got to move? Why didn't someone tell us earlier?"

Joe empathized with the foreman, but there was nothing he could do. "I could have told you earlier, but the Twin Valley rig needed me over there for the biggest part of the day."

"I know. I know," Mac said, then waved his hand toward the open door and the muddy ground outside. "But what's the matter with this spot? From what the geologist said we'll find gas anywhere we sink a hole around here."

"I've read the reports and he's right. You would find gas here, but I doubt you'd ever get it out of the ground."

"Why?" asked the crewman who'd so far been silent.

"Rock," Joe answered flatly.

"Damn," Mac cursed, "we deal with rock all the time. We'll drill around the stuff, or go at an angle."

"Not in this case," Joe replied. "There's a solid ledge of it, running a good three hundred feet down. If we drill here we're gonna have nothing but hell to go through."

The foreman cursed while the other two men groaned.

"Look, Joe, I know that you're the boss, but you can't know there's rock like that right here. Even the geologist won't know that for sure until we start to drill and pull up ground samples."

Joe's blue eyes turned steely. "I *am* a geologist, Mac. And a damned good one! Don't try to tell *me* what's under this ground!"

All three crewmen stared at Joe as if he were someone they'd never met before instead of their boss.

"Well, hell, Joe—I wasn't trying to tell you. I didn't know you were a geologist!" Mac exclaimed.

"Forget it," Joe snapped. "You're right, anyway. No one knows what's really under here until the drill bit starts bringing it up. But I've got a gut feeling about this. So go get the rest of the crew and start moving this heap of metal!"

The men jumped to their feet and began grabbing slickers and hard hats. Joe left them and trudged on up the slope until he reached a camp trailer.

Inside he kicked off his muddy boots and sank into a grungy armchair. He needed food and coffee, but he was too tired and disgusted to bother making either one.

Normally Joe preferred this outdoor work to the confines of the office. But not this time. Everything had seemed to be going wrong. And it was hard to concentrate on problems when Savanna was all he could think about.

As he waited for the coffee to boil on the small propane cookstove, he pulled the blinds on the window and looked out at the miserable weather. Rain was still falling steadily, turning the newly excavated earth into a bog of red mush.

Oklahoma rarely saw this much rain in June. In fact, when he'd left early this morning, Oklahoma City had been clear and dry. But for some reason a band of thunderheads had decided to spill their guts right over Rig 243, or, more aptly named, Rock Ridge.

Face it, Joe, it's not the rain that's bothering you, a voice sounded in his head. And it's not the wasted time and manpower of moving the rat hole. It was Savanna.

He hadn't even been gone a whole day and already he missed her. He never thought he'd ever feel this way about a woman. Especially after his failed marriage to Deirdre. But Savanna had somehow gotten into his blood and he didn't know how to get her out. Or even if he wanted to.

Hell, Joe, you want to get her in bed, that's all, the voice continued. Groaning aloud, Joe glanced at the coffeepot. It wasn't boiling yet. But his thoughts were.

He didn't just want to make love to Savanna, he argued with himself as he walked over to the far end of the room and pulled off his wet shirt. Yesterday in the office, when he'd had her in his arms, he'd felt more than just hot lust.

All sorts of soft, protective feelings had jumbled themselves up with the physical urge to be close to her. And later, when he'd come home and sat chatting with Megan at the supper table, it was as if something had been missing. And he'd realized it was Savanna.

Closing his eyes in desperation, he blotted the rain from his shoulders and chest with the dirty shirt, then tossed it on the floor.

Joe didn't want a wife. And Savanna didn't want a lover. So what was he going to do? Just forget her? Yeah, he thought grimly. There was about as much chance of that as him forgetting how to breathe.

He'd barely poured his coffee when a voice interrupted. "Joe! Mr. McCann! Are you in there?"

Joe looked around just as one of the hands burst through the door. His face was deathly white even though he'd obviously been running.

"What's the matter?" Joe asked quickly.

"It's Mac," he blurted between gasps for air. "He's fallen. I think he's hurt bad."

Not bothering with a shirt, Joe jerked on his boots, then motioned for the worker to precede him out the door.

"What happened? Where is he?" Joe fired the questions at the young man as the two of them hurried across the muddy site.

"Over by the derrick. He was trying to loosen a cable or something. I don't know. I just heard him yell and then I looked around and saw him facedown on the ground."

By the time they reached Mac, the rest of the concerned crew had crowded around the injured man. They parted immediately to let Joe through. He squatted on his heels and touched the foreman's shoulder. "Mac, can you hear me?"

When he failed to get a response, Joe felt along the side of his neck for a pulse.

"Is he breathing?" someone asked.

"I don't—" Before Joe could finish the sentence, Mac let out a low groan. Joe lowered his ear to Mac's mouth.

"Get—me up," he gasped weakly.

"No. You're not to move!" he told the foreman, then yelled over his shoulder. "Robert, get on the phone in my truck!"

"Do they have 911 here?" the young worker asked.

"Hell, I don't know! Call the sheriff's office. I doubt an ambulance could make it back in here, anyway. We'll probably have to haul him out to the nearest county road. Now go!"

Robert raced away and Joe turned back to the older man. "Hang on, Mac," he said urgently. "We're going to get you out of here."

In the end, Joe was right. The mountain road was too rough for an ambulance. In order to protect his neck and back the men carefully loaded Mac onto a sheet of plyboard then pushed him into the back of Joe's pickup.

Joe climbed in with him and motioned for the driver to head down the mountain.

As they rocked slowly over the rough road, Joe did his best to keep Mac talking and alert. "Mac, you're getting soft," Joe told the injured man. "This looks more like a log trail than a rig road. What the heck did you do, give the grader man a paid vacation?"

Mac tried to smile but it came off more like a grimace. "I didn't know—I—I'd be coming over it like this."

Joe struggled to laugh, but the sound that came out of his throat sounded more like a frog croaking. In that moment he wished Savanna was here beside him. She'd know just what to say to Mac to keep him going. She'd be able to laugh and smile and assure him that everything was going to be all right.

"Where do you hurt, Mac?"

"My chest," he whispered. "Can't breathe."

"You'll be fine. It's probably just a broken rib or two."

"I—don't know, Joe. It hurts like hell."

Joe looked through the back windshield to the road up ahead of them. At this snail's pace they were never going to make it to the county road.

Mac shook his head. "Joe, I—if I don't make it—"

"I don't want to hear any of that," Joe interrupted. "You'll be back on the job in a week."

"No, Joe. Listen, I want you to tell my wife—" He drew in a weak breath, shuddering with the effort. "Tell her how much I love her. She's my life. Her and the kids. They're all that matter to me. Tell them that."

Joe nodded. "I will."

Mac closed his eyes and was silent for so long that a chill of fear washed over Joe. "Mac?"

Finally Mac drew in another painful breath and said, "A man can lose lots of things, Joe. But if he loses his family—that's what ruins him. You remember that. You hear me?"

Joe grabbed Mac's rough hand and squeezed it. "Yeah. I hear you, buddy. I hear you. But I'm not going to let you die. I'm going to get you back to that wife of yours."

"McCann Drilling." Savanna spoke cheerfully into the receiver. "May I help you?"

"Yeah, girl, you sure can. Do you deliver gas? I'm on the freeway and it's a long walk to the nearest station."

"Daddy," she said, laughing as she recognized his thinly disguised voice. "What are you doing?"

"Oh, I just got home from work and Gloria is about to start supper. We thought you might want to come over and eat when you get off there."

"That's nice of you, Daddy, but I'm afraid I can't. I'm tied up tonight."

"Oh," he said slyly. "Have you finally gotten around to finding a date?"

Savanna groaned. "No. Actually, I'm baby-sitting my boss's daughter. He's been out of town the past two days."

Thurman chuckled. "Getting in a little overtime, are you? I guess you'll have plenty of rent money this month."

"Oh, I'm not charging Joe. This is just something I wanted to do. Megan, his daughter, is... Well, her mother lives in Africa and her daddy is—"

"Your boss," Thurman finished in a pointed tone.

Savanna tapped her pencil against the open ledger book. "That doesn't mean anything," she said defensively.

"I didn't say it did," Thurman retorted. "I know nothing about the man. Except what you told us. Is he still making you nervous?"

Savanna very nearly laughed in her father's ear. What Joe did to her went far beyond nervous.

Glancing over at his empty desk, she said, "I've learned a lot about him these past few days. He's not the man I thought he was that first day I met him."

Thurman was silent for a long time and Savanna got the impression he wanted to ask her more about Joe. But when he did finally speak it was about something entirely different.

"I guess I should tell you that my job here at Sooner Insurance has just about wound up. Looks like we'll be leaving in a couple of weeks. Next stop New Orleans."

"Oh, I'm sorry," Savanna said.

"Are you kidding? I've always wanted to visit the French Quarter and eat gumbo."

"No, I meant I'm going to be sorry to see you and Gloria leave. You're the only family I've got, you know."

"Sweetheart, I'll only be a phone call away."

"I know. But it would be nice if you were staying here," Savanna said with a sigh, then tossed down the pencil and rubbed her forehead. Suddenly she felt more alone than she ever had in her life.

"Five more years and then I'll be able to retire and sink roots. But it's your time now, honey. You need to start making some roots of your own."

"I will if I can, Daddy."

Laughing, Thurman scoffed at the doubt in her voice. "Don't give me that half-try attitude, Savanna. You've always been a cockeyed optimist. And I have a feeling by the time I retire you'll have some grandchildren to keep me busy."

Later that evening as Savanna drove to Joe's house, she mulled over the conversation she'd had with her father. Strange that he'd called her a cockeyed optimist. Joe had called her the very same thing. Yet she hardly felt like one. It seemed to Savanna that her life was splintering in all different directions and if she didn't get control, everything she'd ever dreamed and hoped for was going to be in shambles.

As far as her giving him grandchildren was concerned, well, she was going to tell her father not to hold his breath. She couldn't imagine herself having any man's child. Unless that man was Joe.

The thought came out of nowhere and stunned her with its implications. Had some deep part of her already decided she wanted to have a child with Joe? That was crazy! Joe didn't want to be a husband again, much less father another child. And even if he did, she wasn't about to let herself dream that she could be a part of his life.

Chapter Eleven

It was past midnight when Joe stepped onto the porch and unlocked the front door. He'd been driving for over two and a half hours and he couldn't remember a time he'd ever felt this exhausted or more glad to be home.

Inside the foyer the dim glow of a lamp shone from the direction of the living room. With a sigh and a tired shrug of his shoulders, Joe went to turn it off.

Yet before he got halfway into the room his feet came to an abrupt halt. Savanna was lying asleep on one of the couches. Her left arm was dangling off the edge of the cushion. Just below her fingers a book lay open on the floor.

The sight of her filled Joe with such a surge of emotion a lump formed in his throat and all he could do was stand and look at her.

But after a while the need to be closer propelled him to take the last few steps to the couch, where he squatted on his heels and eased the book from beneath her lifeless fingers.

Corporate Taxes. No wonder she'd fallen asleep, he thought as he glanced at the title.

Joe put the book down by the lamp on the end table, then gazed down at her sleeping face. It had been scrubbed free of makeup and her hair was brushed back from her brow. She was wearing a pair of white satin pajamas. The neckline was gaping, exposing the top of one breast.

It was all Joe could do to keep from reaching out with one finger, pushing the soft, slinky fabric just an inch farther and exposing her dusky pink nipple.

"Savanna?"

She didn't stir at the sound of his voice. Joe tried again, this time touching her shoulder. After a moment her eyelids fluttered open and she stared blankly up at him.

"Joe?"

Her voice was husky and full of surprise. The sound of it sent a wave of longing spiraling through him.

"Yes. It's me."

She closed her eyes, then pressed the heels of her hands against them. "I guess I fell asleep while I was reading."

"Maybe you should try a thriller next time, instead of IRS regulations."

She dropped her hand and looked at him. The wry grin on his face woke her faster than anything could have.

"What—what are you doing home at this hour? We thought you wouldn't be back until tomorrow afternoon."

Easing down beside her, he let his eyes travel slowly, longingly over her flushed cheeks, sleepy eyes and soft full lips. He'd never get enough of looking at her, he realized.

"I'd intended to wait and drive home tomorrow. But my plans changed."

There was an odd rawness to his voice, an unfamiliar vulnerableness on his face that told Savanna she was seeing an entirely different Joe than the one who'd left nearly two days ago.

Pushing herself to a sitting position, she laid her hand on his arms. "Joe, is—something wrong?"

The concern in her voice went straight to his heart and filled him with a burgeoning need to hold her, tell her just how much she meant to him.

"No. Yes. I—"

He didn't finish. He couldn't finish. There were no words to tell her all the things that had passed through his mind since he'd been away.

"Oh, Savanna, Savanna," he whispered, his voice a strange mixture of awe and anguish. "I'm so glad you're here."

Confusion filled her eyes. "I'm—glad I'm here, too," she said softly.

Was she? he wondered. Was she aching to touch him, hold him, love him the way he ached to love her?

"I hope so, Savanna. Because I can't—"

He stopped abruptly, making Savanna's brows lift in question.

"Can't what?" she prompted, her heart beating rapidly in her throat.

His answer was a low groan and before Savanna realized what was happening, her head was lying in the crook of his arm and his lips were making a hot, hungry search of hers.

Savanna didn't resist. She kissed him back. It was the only thing her heart would allow her to do.

Long moments later Joe finally tore his lips from hers and lifted his head. By then his breathing was raspy and Savanna felt close to fainting.

"Joe, have you gone crazy?" she whispered.

A wan smile moved over his face. "No. I've just now come to my senses."

As Savanna tried to figure out what he meant by that, his head bent toward hers again. However, this time she put her hands against his chest and held him at bay. There were too many questions she wanted answered and she didn't want to give him the chance of seducing her before she asked them.

"What is that supposed to mean?" she asked, then, wriggling out of his arms, she scooted down to the end of the couch.

Joe slid down the slick leather after her. "It means I've come to some conclusions about you. And me."

Her expression wary, she studied his face. "You and me? Look Joe, the other day in the office—"

"I wanted you like I've never wanted any woman in my life," he finished for her.

Her cheeks full of heat, she said, "You showed me that much."

His blue eyes darkened as he leaned closer and murmured, "I want to show you again, Savanna."

Her heart pounding like a runaway engine, Savanna jumped to her feet and crossed the room. "Joe, I told you—"

"I know what you told me." Rising to his feet, he went to her. Savanna trembled like an aspen leaf in the wind as his hands framed her face and his eyes delved into hers. "You told me you need more than just sex. Well, so do I, Savanna. I realize that now. Among other things."

"Other things?" she whispered dizzily.

Suddenly he was groaning, tugging her into his arms and burying his face against the side of her neck.

"I love you, Savanna. I love you."

Savanna's head swirled with shock. What was he saying? He loved her? Really loved her? No, that was just too much to believe.

"Joe, I—don't think..."

He drew his head back far enough to enable him to see her face. Savanna drew in a deep breath and tried to go on. "Am I supposed to believe that? You think saying you love me is going to make me go to bed with you?"

Joe put his hands on her shoulders and held on tightly. "No, I think it's going to make you marry me."

Savanna had only thought she'd been shocked by his vows of love. This utterly stunned her.

"Marry you?" she gasped, then, as if putting the distance between them would keep her safe, she whirled away from his grasp and hurried to the far end of the room to stand by the fireplace. "You don't want to marry any woman. Much less me! Have you gone mad, or what? I think you've been working in a loony bin instead of a rig site!"

To her amazement, Joe laughed. "Nope. I'm sane and sober. And," he added, his expression going serious, "I want to marry you."

How could those words make her so happy and frightened at the same time? Savanna wondered.

Her head shook back and forth with total disbelief. "Don't you think this is all rather sudden? A few days ago you insisted, vehemently if I remember right, that you never wanted to marry again. Ever. No matter who the woman was."

Joe crossed the room to her. Still numb with shock, Savanna allowed him to lead her over to one of the couches. Once the two of them had taken a seat on the edge of the cushion, he reached for her hands and slid his fingers intimately between hers.

"I know it all seems sudden—"

"Joe," she quickly interrupted, "a person just doesn't make an abrupt about-face like this without a good reason."

Annoyed, he frowned and asked, "What difference does it make why I've changed my mind about marriage?"

She looked incredulous. "Joe, for a man who has always lived a controlled life, you're certainly stepping out of character now."

He released one of her hands and swiped his fingers through his hair. It was then that Savanna noticed his bloodshot eyes and the deep lines of fatigue on his face.

Suddenly a part of her wanted to pull his head against her breast, hold him and tell him how much she adored him. But to do that would be like forfeiting everything she'd worked for the past five years. Independence, freedom, peace of mind. How could she give all that up? Why would she even want to? Because you love him, a little voice inside her answered.

"Maybe I've just now learned who my character really is," Joe went on.

Her expression full of doubt, she said, "The other day you seemed to be pretty sure of that. You're Joe Oilman McCann. And that's all you want to be."

Joe shook his head. "I'm Megan's father. And I want to be your husband."

She didn't say anything and Joe got the impression she was waiting for him to go on, that he hadn't said nearly enough to convince her that his feelings were genuine.

With a groan of frustration he said, "Look, Savanna, my foreman was seriously injured yesterday on the job. He fell from the derrick and I thought he— Well, I thought he was going to die before we could get him out to the nearest hospital."

Savanna suddenly hurt for Joe and the man she'd never met. "He didn't. Did he?" she asked anxiously.

Joe shook his head. "No, thank God. Both of his lungs were punctured with broken ribs, along with a broken wrist and collarbone. But he's going to be all right."

"I'm glad," Savanna said.

"No gladder than I," Joe told her. "During that slow drive out of the mountains—" He stopped, swallowed, then closed his eyes. "I didn't think he was going to make it. I truly believe the only reason he survived is because he didn't want to leave his wife or children."

The anguish on Joe's face compelled Savanna to reach out and touch his face, soothe away the fear he must have endured. "Oh, God, Joe, I'm so sorry," she said, and truly meant it. "That must have been like reliving a nightmare. You probably saw your father dying all over again."

Joe nodded, then pulled her hand away from his cheek and brought the palm up to his lips. Savanna nearly groaned as a rush of bittersweet emotions tore through her body. She loved this man and now he was telling her he loved her, too.

But love didn't come with an insurance policy, she silently reminded herself. And she was desperately afraid that if she dared even think of having a future with Joe it would ruin both their lives.

"The whole thing made me realize how much you and Megan mean to me, Savanna. Do you believe me now?"

A part of her wanted to believe, to dream that she could be his wife and the mother of his children. But that wasn't the safe, common sense thing to do.

"I don't know, Joe. I—" Turning her head away from him, she bit down on her lip and prayed the tears at the back of her eyes would go away. "Even if you did love me . . ."

His hand closed over her chin and pulled her face back around to him. "There's no ifs about it, Savanna. I do love you. Now all I want to know is whether you love me."

Savanna's first instinct was to lie, to say she had no feelings for him whatsoever. But lying wouldn't solve her problem. As far as she could see, nothing would.

"That really doesn't matter," she said in a choked voice, then, fearing she was going to break into sobs, she got to her feet and rushed out to the kitchen.

Joe quickly followed and watched from the doorway as she took down a glass from the cabinet and filled it with cold water from the refrigerator. All the while keeping her back to him.

Bewildered by her behavior, Joe said, "I don't understand you, Savanna. I just laid my heart out on the table for you and you want to take a carving knife and cut it into tiny little pieces."

Doing her best to swallow down the hot lump in her throat, Savanna turned away from the sink to look at him, then wished she hadn't. There was genuine pain on his face and she was the cause of it. But it was better to hurt him now than later, she fiercely told herself.

Placing the glass on the table, she went to him and this time she didn't try to hide her feelings. The love she felt for him was on her face and in the touch of her hand as she laid it gently against his heart.

"Okay, Joe. You want the truth, I'll tell you the truth. I think I fell in love with you the first day I went to work for you."

"I was terrible to you that day!" he exclaimed.

In spite of the anguish she was feeling, a wan smile curved her lips. "I won't argue with you there. But you said you needed me. I'd never had a boss tell me that before."

Amazed, he said, "I just hope you've never had a boss propose to you before."

"Oh, I can assure you that you're the first man to get that close—" She broke off as red-hot heat filled her cheeks. "Well, you're the first boss I ever kissed."

"I wish I'd known how you felt. Why didn't you tell me?"

Savanna's lips twisted with regret. "It wouldn't have served any purpose to tell you. You ought to know how I feel. I'm jinxed where marriage is concerned. I've had to accept that having a family is for other people, not for me. Besides," she added, her eyes dropping to the floor, "things could never work for us."

Groaning, he turned his eyes toward the ceiling. "How can you say that? You're the one who's been preaching that a person should go after what they want!"

Savanna absently studied his mud-caked boots and jeans. "You don't want me," she said wearily. "Not really. Yesterday you saw your friend nearly die and it reminded you of your own mortality. That's all."

"Hellfire, Savanna! I know I'm going to die. Someday. We all are. I want to live with you, love with you before that happens."

She finally found the courage to lift her eyes back to his and she looked at him with wry resignation. "Maybe a part of you does. A little part. The other part of you is married to McCann Drilling. Just like your father, Joseph, was."

His blue eyes suddenly blazed with anger. "I'm not married to McCann's! All I'm trying to do is keep the damn thing running!"

She shot him a hopeless look, then turned and walked out of the kitchen and down the hallway.

Just as she was about to reach her bedroom door, Joe's hand caught her shoulder and spun her back around to him. She stared at him, her heart pounding sickly in her breast, her eyes daring him to say anything to prove her wrong.

"Savanna," he said more calmly. "McCann's is my job. That's all. A man has to have a job. Whether I'm an oil field man or not has nothing to do with you becoming my wife."

Knowing there wasn't anything else she could say to get through to him, she threw up her hands in a helpless gesture. "If you think of McCann's as just a job, then I know there is absolutely no hope that we could ever have a future together."

She started to pull out of his grasp, but his hold tightened on her shoulder. "Why?" he demanded.

Did he honestly not know? Savanna wondered. "Because running the company is making you miserable. Even Megan can see that. Yet you spend all your time on it."

"I wouldn't neglect either of you," he assured her.

"I wasn't implying you would. But if you're not happy now, how can you honestly expect our marriage to be any better?"

Breathing deeply, Joe reached out with his other hand and drew her head against his chest. "Because you would make me happy," he said simply.

With her cheek pressed to his heart and his arms wrapped warmly around her, she desperately wanted to believe him. But she'd trusted and lost in the past. She was terrified it would happen again.

"I can't think about this tonight, Joe," she said tiredly. "I'm going home."

He eased her head back. "Tonight? No! I don't want you driving out on the streets at this hour. And Megan won't understand if she wakes up and finds you've gone."

He was right, and she wouldn't want to hurt Megan for any reason. Easing out of his embrace, she said, "All right, I'll stay for her sake."

Joe reached over and opened her bedroom door, then touching her cheek, he whispered, "I wish you were staying for my sake, too."

Savanna couldn't say anything. Joe loved her. She should be shouting with joy. Instead, her heart was shattering with pain and regret.

"Good night," she choked through her tears, then hurried inside her bedroom and foolishly locked the door behind her. As if she could ever lock him out of her heart.

Chapter Twelve

Joe had already gone to work when Savanna rose the next morning. By the time she shared breakfast with Megan then drove to the office, he was gone from there, too.

With a mixture of relief and disappointment, Savanna read a note, she found on her desk.

Savanna,
Sorry I missed you this morning, but there's been some equipment trouble and I had to leave early. We'll *talk* tonight.

Love, Joe

So that meant he was probably going to be out of the office all day, Savanna concluded as she folded the note and tossed it to one side of her desk. It was probably just as well that he wasn't going to be here tempting her, trying to persuade her to marry him.

We'll talk tonight. What was he going to say that he hadn't already said? And how was she going to convince him that she didn't want to marry him? For that matter, how was she going to convince herself?

The day turned into a long one for Savanna. Without Joe around there was little work for her to do. She typed what few letters she could without his approval, then posted a small stack of bills to the ledger sheet.

Megan called her twice to ask if she'd be coming back to see her tonight. Both times Savanna had put her off as gently as possible. The girl needed companionship with someone who was going to be a permanent fixture in her life. Not someone like Savanna, who was only a temporary stand-in mom.

All her life she'd been a temporary everything, she thought sadly. A temporary friend, secretary, fiancée. The only constant role she'd ever held was daughter. And even that was going to be on a long-distance basis now that her father and stepmother were going to be moving to New Orleans. Savanna had never felt more alone or lost.

The sun was still high and hot at five that evening when Savanna closed the office and climbed into her Volkswagen. She rolled down the windows and started the engine as quickly as she could. Without an air conditioner to cool the interior, she wanted to get to her apartment and out of the heat as fast as possible.

She was backing out of the parking slot when Joe's pickup suddenly pulled to a stop directly behind her. Savanna jammed on the brakes and waited for him to come to her.

"I've already locked the office," she told him as he approached her car. "Do you need for me to unlock it? I still have the key you gave me."

"No, I just came by to catch you before you left." He leaned his head in the window, then, with a cocky smile she'd never seen on him before, he planted a kiss on her mouth. "Did you have any problems today?"

No problems with work, she thought. Just a major struggle to keep him out of her head. And what little progress she'd made at that had just crumbled beneath his kiss.

"Everything was slow. Although you did get a call from a potential client. He has a lease in the southeast part of the state to be drilled and he thinks McCann's is the company he wants to do it."

"That's good. So are you ready for some supper?"

"You're asking me out?" she asked, her face mirroring her surprise.

He smiled again and Savanna decided the ordeal he'd gone through with his foreman had definitely done something to him. This was a different Joe, an almost happy Joe!

"Since I've already asked you to marry me, I might as well ask you out to supper."

Her first instinct was to refuse. But he obviously wanted to talk to her and it wouldn't make much difference if their conversation was over the evening meal or over the phone. The outcome was going to be the same. She couldn't marry Joe.

"What about Megan? Is she coming with us?"

He shook his head. "I've already explained to her where we'll be. Anyway, she's all excited because I'm letting her go to the movies with Cindy."

"The girl across the street?" Savanna was amazed and it must have shown on her face because he smiled and shrugged.

"I'm not a complete ogre, Savanna. Now kill that orange thing and let's get out of here."

Minutes later they entered a quiet little French café on the opposite side of town. Expecting to be eating at a fast-food joint or steak house, Savanna looked around with mild surprise at the quaint but elegant tables.

"You had to make reservations for this," Savanna said after the waiter had seated them and Joe had ordered a bottle of wine. "Why didn't we go to that fast food place?"

"McCann Drilling might be close to bankruptcy, but I'm not. I can afford to feed you a good dinner."

"I wasn't implying that you couldn't afford it. I just... don't want you to waste your money on me."

Frowning, he picked up the menu and opened it. "I'm not a teenager, Savanna. I don't expect sex for repayment of a meal."

"You know," she said pleasantly as she leaned back in her chair, "I don't think I've ever struck anyone in my life. But I constantly get the urge to pick something up and bop you over the head with it. I wonder what that means? That I've got a violent streak in me that I didn't know about?"

He put the wine list aside and looked at her. "It means you love me."

His words caught her completely off guard and it was a moment or two before she could respond. "What makes you think so?"

"Because love and hate are just like that." Holding up his hands he pressed his palms flat against each other. "You can't have one without the other."

"I hardly expected you to have an opinion on the subject," she admitted truthfully. "Is that what was wrong with you and Deirdre. You didn't have the right mixture of love and hate?"

Before he could answer the waiter returned with the wine. After he filled their glasses and left, Joe turned back to Savanna. "Deirdre didn't have the nerve or urge to bop anybody. She was as placid as a milquetoast. There wasn't a really passionate bone in her body."

"She sounds perfect for you," Savanna couldn't help saying.

He laughed, then shook his head. "Deirdre and I bored each other to tears. She thought I was a stuffed-shirt scientist and I thought she was a clinging whiner."

"Dear Lord, why did you ever marry her in the first place?"

"I thought milquetoast would be easier to digest than something spicy. And I guess it was like Megan said, I needed to rebel against Joseph. And marrying Deirdre was the way to do it. God, what a mistake," he added in afterthought.

"Deirdre was obviously a mistake," Savanna told him. "But the rebellion against your father wasn't. I wish you'd done more of it."

"You don't like him, do you?" he asked.

She looked at him over the rim of her wine goblet. "Your father?" When he nodded, she went on, "I don't even know him. Besides, he's no longer living."

"Even so, you don't like his image."

She swallowed a sip of the wine in hopes it would give her enough courage to hold her senses together. "No. I don't like Joseph McCann. He took away your childhood. He took away your right to be your own person. Most of all, he took away your happiness."

"I'm happy."

"Really?" she asked, the sarcasm in her voice telling him how much she believed him.

"I will be when you marry me."

She looked away from him and sadly shook her head. "And you think I'm going to make everything all right? That having me in your life is going to make you happy?"

"Why not?"

She leaned toward him then and tightly clasped his hand between the two of hers. "Because I believe with all my heart that you're never going to be truly happy until you turn the reins of McCann's over to someone else."

"Savanna, I—" he began the warning, only to have her interrupt.

"You're a geologist, Joe! I know that's what you really want to be doing. Not sitting behind a desk or meeting with money men. You want to be out in the field doing exploration work. Admit it. Can't you?"

It was only a few days ago that he'd been able to admit it to himself, much less to someone else, Joe thought. But Savanna had done something to him and he was no longer that same Joe who couldn't talk or laugh or smile.

"You're right, Savanna. Totally right. But that doesn't change things. I may want to work as a geologist again, but I can't. What a person wants and what he is obligated to do are two different things."

The expectant, hopeful expression fell from Savanna's face and she released his hand.

"I guess you're right, Joe," she said flatly. "And five years ago I obligated myself to a career in accounting. I'm going to stick to it. I'm going back to college, get my degree and start a CPA business of my own."

Joe's eyes took in her jutted chin, the arch of her neck and the small gold locket nestled between her breasts. She was gorgeous and spirited and passionate and nothing like a milquetoast. And he wanted her more than anything he'd ever wanted in his life.

"That's good. You can work as my CPA. I'm always having to call one in at McCann's."

Savanna slowly shook her head. "I don't think so." Her eyes caught his and begged him to understand. "I haven't changed my mind since last night, Joe. I'm not going to marry you."

"Savanna, you—"

To Joe's annoyance the waiter came up just at that moment to take their orders. After he'd finally left, Joe leaned across the table to Savanna, his eyes dark and intense. "Why? Just tell me that. Or can you?"

"Why? Damn it, Joe," she retorted, then glanced around to make sure there were no other diners close enough to hear her. "I don't want you to be my next Bruce, or my next Terry. I can't go through that again. And don't ask me to," she tacked on the moment she saw his mouth fly open.

"What do you want us to do? Simply go back to work tomorrow and act as though we're just employee and employer?"

"It would be a great relief to me."

He wanted to marry her and spend the rest of his life with her and all she wanted was relief! He wanted to shake her, kiss her, yell some sort of sense into her.

"Fine," he said angrily. "Anything to make you happy, Ms. Starr!"

The remainder of the meal was spent in total silence. Even the trip back to McCann's to pick up her car was made with a minimal amount of words.

When he finally pulled to a stop beside her Volkswagen, Savanna exhaled a deep sigh of relief.

"Thank you for supper," she said stiffly. "The food was delicious."

She'd hardly touched it, Joe thought. But what the hell, she didn't want to touch him, either.

"You're welcome," he said trying his best to sound as cool as she had.

Savanna nodded, then hastily reached for the door handle.

"Savanna?"

Her heart pounding, she looked over at him. "What?"

His answer was to reach for her and drag her across the seat and into his arms.

"What are you doing?" she muttered as his mouth lowered to hers.

"I want to give you something to think about tomorrow. When we go back to being employer and employee," he murmured, then, closing the last fraction between their lips, he kissed her as he had that day in the office when she'd practically begged him to make love to her.

Desire swamped Savanna and for long moments all she could do was want more.

Then suddenly he was putting her away from him. "Good night, Savanna."

He leaned across her and opened the door. She didn't say anything and Joe watched her scramble to the ground and quickly climb into the Volkswagen. Once she'd gunned the engine to life, she reversed away from his truck and sped off into the darkness without a backward glance.

Yet it was a long time before Joe started his own truck and left McCann's parking lot. And even then his hands were still shaking. Life without Savanna wasn't going to be any sort of life at all. What was he going to do to make her see that?

Savanna unlocked the door to her apartment, then with a sigh of relief stepped into the cool interior. The temperature had been blistering hot for the past two weeks and it looked as though there was no relief in sight.

Tossing her purse onto a low coffee table, Savanna walked into her bedroom and quickly stripped off the white linen dress she'd worn to work, then pulled on a pair of red jersey shorts and matching T-shirt.

The heat was definitely getting to her. Every evening she came home from work totally exhausted and her head throbbing like a bass drum. She was going to have to do something about getting an air conditioner installed in her car or buying a vehicle that already had one.

Who are you kidding, Savanna? she asked herself, as she stood before the dresser and pulled a brush through her short hair. The heat wasn't the reason she wanted to burst into tears every five minutes. It was Joe.

He'd rarely spoken to her these past two weeks. But then she supposed there wasn't much he could say that he hadn't already. And there wasn't much she could say either, she thought glumly. She'd made her choice. Now she had to stick with it.

But it was breaking her heart into pieces and she didn't know what to do about it.

A knock at the door had her tossing down her hairbrush and hurrying out to the living room.

Relieved to see Jenny on the other side of the door, Savanna grabbed her friend by the hand and welcomed her into the apartment.

"Well, it's been a while since anyone has acted this glad to see me," Jenny said as Savanna ushered her into the living area. "Not too many people are happy to find a cop at their door."

With a wan smile, Savanna said, "I'm very glad to see you. In fact, I've been wondering why you haven't been over for a visit."

Sinking wearily down on the end of the couch, Savanna motioned for Jenny to take a seat.

"I've been working," the redhead said. "A summer flu bug has been going around in the department. I've had to

work double shifts, then grab as much sleep as I can in between."

"Well, the work must be agreeing with you. You look
lovely."

Jenny waved away the compliment. "I wish I could say
the same for you, but you look awful. What's the matter?
Is your job nearly over?"

Savanna pressed her fingertips against her forehead. "No.
Not yet. But Edie had her baby last week and since they're
both doing fine, I don't expect my services will be needed for
too much longer."

Jenny's expression turned to one of concern as she heard
the painful wobble in Savanna's voice.

"And you don't want to quit working for Joe?" she
asked.

"Frankly, Jenny, I don't think I can take it much longer."
With a heavy sigh Savanna rubbed her throbbing temples.
Across the room Jenny kicked off her flats and drew her legs
up beneath her. The two women hadn't visited since the
night they'd gone shopping at the mall. More than two
weeks had passed since then. Two weeks of hell as far as
Savanna was concerned.

"Okay, tell me all about it, honey. You've gone and fallen
in love with the guy, haven't you?"

Savanna moaned and pressed her fingers tighter against
her forehead. "How did you guess?"

Jenny laughed. "By the miserable expression on your
face. Only a man can make a woman look the way you do."

Tears filled Savanna's eyes and she swiped at them angrily. She'd never been a crier. But this past week her tears
had never been far from the surface.

"I just—don't know what to do, Jenny. The office is like
a deep freeze. We don't say anything to each other unless we
have to. And all because..."

"Because of what?" Jenny prompted.

Savanna sniffed and looked over at her friend. "I won't agree to marry him."

In a flash Jenny was out of her chair and sitting beside Savanna.

"Are you telling me the man has proposed to you?" she asked incredulously.

Her face glum, Savanna nodded. "I had to tell him no. And he doesn't understand why."

"Well, frankly, neither can I," Jenny said after a moment.

Puzzled, Savanna stared at her. "You think I should have said yes? You, of all people! Man hater Jenny thinks I should get married?"

Laughing, Jenny nodded. "I don't hate men. Especially one that sounds as sexy as your Joe McCann."

"Joe *is* sexy," Savanna reluctantly agreed, "but that doesn't mean I should marry him."

"No. You should marry him because you love him." She carefully studied Savanna's face. "Do you love him? I mean the real kind of love that keeps people together until they're old and gray?"

Savanna desperately raked her fingers through her hair. "I've asked myself that over and over for the past two weeks," she said, her voice full of anguish.

"And?" Jenny prompted.

Savanna shook her head helplessly and swallowed at the achy knot collecting in her throat. She couldn't lie to Jenny anymore than she could keep lying to herself. "I do love him. I do wish I could be with him until we're both old and gray."

"Then what's the problem? Why don't you accept his proposal?"

Savanna groaned. "Jenny, you know my track record with men. If I agreed to marry Joe, I'd be worried every minute about what was going to happen. Would a lightning bolt come out of the blue and strike him? Or maybe some sultry redhead like you would come along and take him away!"

Jenny shook her head with disbelief. "That's crazy and you know it. Besides, third time is always charmed."

"Jenny, when Terry died I decided that I had to direct my life toward other things. For years now I've concentrated on getting a degree and making a career for myself. I never—" tears filled her eyes and Savanna blinked furiously in an attempt to ward them off "—I didn't mean to fall in love."

"But you have," Jenny said softly. "And why waste your chance for happiness by worrying over things that might never happen?"

Savanna wearily leaned her head back against the cushions. "Maybe nothing bad would happen. But that's not all there is to it. His job is so—well, Joe is a workaholic."

"Aren't a lot of us these days," Jenny said dryly.

"Yes, but Joe hates what he's doing. He's unhappy doing it. How could I ever expect our marriage to survive in that sort of climate?"

"Well, I can certainly tell you one thing—you don't look like a bundle of joy now. Hadn't you rather be unhappy with him than miserable without him?"

Savanna was mulling that over when the doorbell rang. Jenny got to her feet.

"I'll answer it, honey. You just stay there and think about what I said."

Moments later Megan followed the tall redhead into the room. Shocked and pleased to see Joe's daughter, Savanna jumped to her feet. "Megan, what are you doing here?"

An anxious look on her face, she said, "I took a taxi, Savanna. Please don't tell Daddy. He thinks I'm at the library."

"Is something wrong?"

Behind them, Jenny cleared her throat. "I'll be in the kitchen making lemonade, Savanna."

Savanna nodded at the older woman, then led Megan over to the couch.

"Now tell me what's happened," she said once they were seated.

Megan's gaze fell to her lap. "Well, I didn't know why you weren't coming over anymore. So I asked Daddy and he said you had a fight because he asked you to marry him. Is that true?"

"That's pretty much what happened, Megan." She reached over and clasped the young girl's hand. "But I hadn't forgotten you."

Relief flooded the teenager's face. "I'm glad. I thought maybe you wouldn't marry Daddy because of me."

Savanna thought her heart was going to break. "Oh, no, honey. Why would you think that?"

Megan dropped her chin and shrugged one shoulder. "I thought you might just want kids of your own and I'd be in the way."

Savanna reached over and placed her palm against Megan's cheek. "You thought all wrong. I'd be very proud to be your stepmother."

Megan looked at her hopefully. "Then why won't you marry Daddy? He says it's because you're afraid to."

Savanna closed her eyes as a quiet sort of relief settled over her. "I believe your daddy is right. I am very afraid."

"Gee, Savanna, you shouldn't be afraid of Daddy," Megan exclaimed with a shake of her curly head. "I was before I came to live with him. I thought he'd be grouchy and hateful and that it would be horrible to stay in the same house with him all the time. But do you know what?''

Savanna looked down at Megan's blue eyes that were so much like Joe's. "What?" she asked softly.

"I'm not afraid at all anymore. I'm glad I live with Daddy now. Because he was all alone and lonely before I came. And he loves me. He loves you, too, Savanna."

Savanna's eyes filled with tears and she hugged Megan fiercely to her breast. "I know, Megan."

And for the first time Savanna really did know and understand what Joe's love meant to her.

The next morning Savanna dressed in a full-skirted sundress done in tiny beige and white stripes with white high heels, then carefully made up her face. She wanted to look her very best when she told Joe she wanted to marry him.

He was on the telephone when she walked into the office. After giving her a cursory glance, he turned his attention back to the report on his desk.

Savanna tried not to let his cool greeting bother her. She couldn't blame him. She'd gone a little crazy since the night he'd proposed to her. She could only hope he'd understand and forgive her.

While he continued his conversation, Savanna made coffee, then went to her desk to organize the payroll she'd be working on today. Halfway through the stack of time cards, the telephone rang.

Joe was staring at her when she finally hung up the receiver.

"Who was that? You look like you've been talking to a ghost."

Savanna slowly rose to her feet. "That . . . was Edie. She said to tell you that she and the new baby are doing great and she'll be able to come back to work next week."

Rising from his desk, he went over to the coffee machine and turned his back to her. "Well, I'm sure you were happy to hear that. Now you can leave and not be bothered with me or McCann Drilling anymore."

His cold words were more than Savanna's fragile emotions could take. With a little sob she whirled around, covered her face with her hands and prayed she wouldn't cry in front of him. But her prayer went unanswered as hot tears oozed between her fingers and rolled down her cheeks.

"Savanna?"

She couldn't answer and then his voice came from a few inches behind her.

"Are you crying?" he asked with disbelief.

She shook her head and his hands came down on her shoulders. Slowly he turned her around to him.

"You are crying! Why?" he asked gently.

Savanna sniffed and wiped at her cheeks. "I—wanted to look beautiful for you and now I've ruined my face. And—it doesn't matter, anyway. Because you don't even care anymore. And Edie is coming back to take my place."

A comical frown puckered his face. "What? Savanna, you're not making a lick of sense."

She sucked in a deep breath and wiped at another fresh spurt of tears. "I came to work this morning planning to tell you that I... wanted to marry you. But now since Edie—"

Before she could finish, Joe had snatched her up by both shoulders. "You're going to marry me?" he asked, a look of sheer incredulous joy on his face.

Hope rose in her heart as she looked at him. "If you still want me."

"Want you? Dear God, Savanna, do you know how miserable I've been the past few days?"

She shook her head, then groaned with regret. "I've been so crazy, Joe. I knew I loved you. But then when you said you wanted us to get married, I was suddenly terrified. If Megan hadn't come to see me last night—"

"Megan went to see you?"

Savanna nodded, then grabbed hold of both his hands. "Don't be angry at her, Joe. She woke me up, made me see I was behaving just like my mother had. Mom wanted more babies, but she wanted everything to be perfect, all conditions to be right before she jumped in and committed herself. In the end she lost her chance. I don't intend to do that with you, Joe. I don't care if you ever work as a geologist again. I don't care how many wells you drill or don't drill, or even if you have to file bankruptcy on this place. If I make you happy..."

His hands circled her waist and drew her up against him. "You do, my darlin'. Happier than I've ever been in my life."

She smiled up at him through her tears. "Then that's all that matters to me."

Joe's hand awkwardly wiped the tearstains from her cheeks. "I've been doing some thinking, too, Savanna. After Mac was hurt I kept reliving the scene over and over. And I kept comparing it to when my father collapsed."

"Oh, Joe," she pleaded. "Don't torment yourself with all that."

Joe shook his head. "It's all right, Savanna. Because, like you, I can see a lot of things clearly now. When my father was dying he didn't talk of my mother and how she was the light of his life. He didn't even talk to me as a son. His concern wasn't for his wife or child. It was for the company. Finding gas and oil meant more to him than we ever did. And I don't ever want to be like that, Savanna. I'm finally proud to say I'm not the man Joseph McCann was."

Tears of joy slipped from her brown eyes. "I'm proud, too."

"There's something else," he said, a smile suddenly creasing his face. "Yesterday I talked to an old friend in Texas about running the business side of McCann's. If he agrees, and I'm certain he will, I'm going back to my exploration work and handing the head reins over to him."

Savanna couldn't believe what she was hearing. "Joe, you don't have to do this for me."

"I'm doing it for myself, Savanna," he assured her. Leaning his forehead against hers, he whispered, "Now dry those tears, darlin'. I want to see you smile, hear you laugh. It's what I love most about you."

She smiled then, and joy like a light from heaven radiated across her face. "I'm never going to be afraid of loving you, Joe."

For a reply he went over to the door and locked it. Savanna watched, her heart pounding with love and anticipation as he walked back to her and began to unbutton the front of her dress.

"Joe!" Laughing, she caught his fingers in hers. "It's only nine in the morning. Some of the hands are going to be coming after you!"

Giving her a sly wink he went over to his desk and punched a mike button on the two-way radio system. "Dolores, tell the men to take the rest of the day off. With pay. And you, too. Go home and celebrate—your boss is getting married!"

"You don't look like the same man who nearly fired me for being late," she teased when he returned to her.

Joe pulled her into his arms and planted a kiss just below her ear. "I've had lots of lessons since then, Savanna." He lifted his head and his blue eyes glinted sexily back at her. "Speaking of lessons, now that I've learned how to be a daddy to a teenager, what do you say I try my hand with a baby of our own? Or do you think I'm ready for that much of a challenge?''

Sweet, wondrous joy poured into Savanna's heart, filled it until she thought she would burst with happiness.

"I think you'll be a natural," she said. Then, tugging his head down to hers, she gave him a kiss to seal the deal.

*   *   *   *   *

COMING NEXT MONTH

#1090 THE DADDY LIST—Myrna Mackenzie
Fabulous Fathers
Faith Reynolds's little boy longed for a daddy—and she was
determined to find him one. Then her son declared that handsome
widower Nathan Murphy was his first choice. And Faith knew
getting involved with Nathan could mean heartache.

#1091 THE BRIDAL SHOWER—Elizabeth August
Always a Bridesmaid
Emma Wynn was engaged to Mr. Almost-Right, but not if past
love Mike Flint had anything to say about it. He was determined
to find out if their shared passion was truly gone, or merely hidden
deep within her....

#1092 RALEIGH AND THE RANCHER—Laura Anthony
Wranglers and Lace
Daniel McClintock couldn't deny his attraction to Raleigh, his
pretty new ranch hand. But just when Daniel began to dream of
their future, Raleigh's past threatened to drive her away. Would
Daniel be able to show her how to trust in love again?

#1093 BACHELOR BLUES—Carolyn Zane
Confirmed bachelor Cole Richardson treasured his quiet home.
Then Lark St. Clair and her mischievous daughter moved next
door. Now he not only found himself losing his peace and quiet
to this unpredictable pair, but also his heart!

#1094 STRANGER IN HER ARMS—Elizabeth Sites
Presumed dead, his estate dispersed, Alex returned from his ordeal
in the Middle East determined to take back the family home...until
he met Dominique Bellay, the lovely new owner. Now he wanted to
start a new life with both!

#1095 WEDDING BELLS AND DIAPER PINS—Natalie Patrick
Debut Author
On her own, Dani McAdams couldn't win custody of her infant
godson. So when ex-fiancé, Matt Taylor, offered a marriage
of convenience her problems seemed to be solved. Until she
discovered a passion for Matt that made her wish for something
more.

Take 4 bestselling love stories FREE

Plus get a FREE surprise gift!

Special Limited-time Offer

Mail to Silhouette Reader Service™

3010 Walden Avenue
P.O. Box 1867
Buffalo, N.Y. 14269-1867

YES! Please send me 4 free Silhouette Intimate Moments® novels and my free surprise gift. Then send me 6 brand-new novels every month, which I will receive months before they appear in bookstores. Bill me at the low price of $2.89 each plus 25¢ delivery and applicable sales tax, if any.* That's the complete price and a savings of over 10% off the cover prices—quite a bargain! I understand that accepting the books and gift places me under no obligation ever to buy any books. I can always return a shipment and cancel at any time. Even if I never buy another book from Silhouette, the 4 free books and the surprise gift are mine to keep forever.

245 BPA ANRR

Name	(PLEASE PRINT)	
Address	Apt. No.	
City	State	Zip

This offer is limited to one order per household and not valid to present Silhouette Intimate Moments® subscribers. *Terms and prices are subject to change without notice. Sales tax applicable in N.Y.

UMOM-295

He's Too Hot To Handle...but she can take a little heat.

SILHOUETTE

Summer Sizzlers

This summer don't be left in the cold, join Silhouette for the hottest Summer Sizzlers collection. The perfect summer read, on the beach or while vacationing, Summer Sizzlers features sexy heroes who are "Too Hot To Handle." This collection of three new stories is written by bestselling authors Mary Lynn Baxter, Ann Major and Laura Parker.

Available this July wherever Silhouette books are sold.

SS95

SOMETIMES, BIG SURPRISES COME IN SMALL PACKAGES!

Bundles of JOY

MAKE ROOM FOR BABY

by Kristin Morgan A beautiful widow, Camille Boudreaux was content to spend the rest of her life alone. But her peaceful existence was shaken when her only daughter, Skyler, fell in love and married Josh Delacambre, the only son of her first love, Bram. And soon Camille found that not only the pain of their thwarted love still lived, but the passion, as well.... Available in June, only from

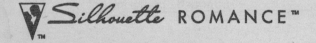

Silhouette ROMANCE™

BOJ2

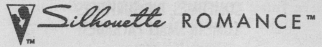 **ROMANCE**™

is proud to present

The spirit of the West—and the magic of romance! Saddle up and get ready to fall in love Western-style with the third installment of WRANGLERS AND LACE. Coming in July with:

Raleigh and the Rancher
by Laura Anthony

Raleigh Travers was wary of love; she had enough on her mind working the ranch and raising her young brother. So when she sensed romantic feelings for rugged Daniel McClintock, the ranch owner, she was careful to keep them to herself. But Raleigh didn't bet on Daniel returning those feelings, or being as bullheaded as a runaway steer in forcing her to acknowledge their passion.

Wranglers and Lace: Hard to tame—impossible to resist—these cowboys meet their match.

In June, get ready for thrilling romances
and FREE BOOKS—Western-style—
with...

WESTERN *Lovers*

You can receive the first 2 Western Lovers titles FREE!

June 1995 brings Harlequin and Silhouette's
WESTERN LOVERS series, which combines larger-than-
life love stories set in the American West! And WESTERN
LOVERS brings you stories with your favorite themes...
"Ranch Rogues," "Hitched In Haste," "Ranchin' Dads,"
"Reunited Hearts" the packaging on each book
highlights the popular theme found in each WESTERN
LOVERS story!

And in June, when you buy either of the Men Made In
America titles, you will receive a WESTERN LOVERS title
absolutely FREE! Look for these fabulous combinations:

◆ Buy ALL IN THE FAMILY
  by Heather Graham Pozzessere (Men Made In
  America) and receive a FREE copy of
  BETRAYED BY LOVE by Diana Palmer
  (Western Lovers)

◆ Buy THE WAITING GAME
  by Jayne Ann Krentz (Men Made In America)
  and receive a FREE copy of
  IN A CLASS BY HIMSELF by JoAnn Ross
  (Western Lovers)

Look for the special, extra-value shrink-wrapped
packages at your favorite retail outlet!

HARLEQUIN®   *Silhouette*®

MAN, WOMAN AND CHILD

Three provocative family tales...three wonderful writers...all come together in a series destined to win your heart! Beginning in June 1995 with

A FATHER'S WISH
by Christine Flynn
SE #962, June

Alexander Burke had never understood why Kelly Shaw had given up their child for adoption. Now she was back...but she didn't know she'd also found the son she thought she'd lost forever.

And don't miss one minute of this innovative series as it continues with these titles:

MOTHER AT HEART
by Robin Elliott
SE #968, July 1995

NOBODY'S CHILD
by Pat Warren
SE #974, August 1995

Only from Silhouette Special Edition!